Nothing
Personal

Nothing
Personal
Jason Starr

FOUR WALLS EIGHT WINDOWS   NO EXIT PRESS

First published in the United States
by Four Walls Eight Windows/No Exit Press
39 West 14th Street, Room 503
New York, NY 10011

www.fourwallseightwindows.com
www.noexit.co.uk

First printing March 2000

ISBN 1-56858-161-0

1   3   5   7   9   8   6   4   2

Typeset by Koinonia, Manchester
and printed and bound in Great Britain

For Sandy

One

JOEY DEPINO WAS the only gambler at the Meadowlands braving the frigid night to watch the last race outside. He was standing by the rail near the finish line in his stone-washed jeans and his blue-and-red New York Giants official team winter jacket. When the white pace car sped past with the long starting gate, he yelled, "Leave with him, Cat Man!" hoping to see his eight horse and Catello Manzi sprinting for the lead. But Manzi was either in on a fix or the damn horse just didn't want to run, because the eight was last, in the middle of the track, looking lame as the pacers rounded the first turn.

"Cocksucker!" Joey screamed.

He tossed his program away over his shoulder and headed toward the grandstand. The bus to Manhattan left at twenty minutes after the last race and he wanted to get a jump on the crowd.

The Meadowlands had been modernized a few years ago, but putting in some snazzy new restaurants and shining up the floors hadn't made much of a difference. The whole place still had a run-down feel to it, mainly because of the crowd. Angry old men,

huddled in small groups, stood cursing at the television
sets that were showing the closed-circuit broadcast of
the race. The floor was covered with losing tickets,
spilled beer, and spit; the air was a haze of cigarette
smoke. At thirty-five, Joey was probably one of the
youngest guys at the track, but years of gambling had
made him look as old and beat-up as everyone else. He
had dark bags under his eyes and most of his hair had
fallen out. He used to lift weights, but that was a long
time ago, when he still lived in Brooklyn; now he
couldn't remember the last time he had set foot in a
gym.

Tonight had cost Joey three hundred and sixty
bucks, not including the price of three hot dogs, two
slices of pizza and one Carvel ice cream cone. But this
was only pocket change compared to the over nine
grand he owed to three bookies and one loan shark.
Because the bookies had stopped taking action from
him, he had started to bet under phony names. But even
"Tony" and "Nick" and "Vinnie" had tapped out their
figures. He had zero money in the bank and with rent
and bills coming up he had no idea what new story he'd
make up to tell his wife Maureen.

At a television set above the betting windows, Joey
stopped to watch the end of the race. His horse still
wasn't in the picture. He couldn't remember the last
time he'd left a racetrack with money in his wallet. Was
it last month? Last year? He felt numb and exhausted; it
seemed like he hadn't had a good night's sleep in
months.

As the pacers turned into the stretch, the eight
finally appeared on the screen. Manzi was moving the
horse up on the rail, but seemed hopelessly boxed-in. In
the stretch, he angled the horse off the rail, then he got

shut off again. He dropped back on the inside, but he was still blocked. Joey was ready to walk away when Manzi somehow got loose. He steered the horse to the outside and started closing like a freight train. It still didn't look like he'd get up in time, but the horse in front was staggering. Joey didn't even have time to scream. Manzi's horse seemed to be moving twice as fast as the other horses, and he surged to the lead at the wire. It would be a photo finish but it was obvious that the eight had won the race.

In an instant, Joey calculated his winnings. At sixty-five to one, the eight was the second longest shot in the field. He had bet forty dollars to win and had played the eight in a forty dollar daily double with the winner of the last race. All together, he would get back over $17,600.

He was too shocked to celebrate. He walked around the grandstand, breathing heavily, hoping he wouldn't have a heart attack and die with the winning tickets in his pocket. He still couldn't believe the eight had actually won. Joey DePino, the guy his friends in Brooklyn used to call "Joey the Jinx" because he always lost at the track, actually getting home a sixty-five-to-one shot? There had to be some mistake. This was "Candid Camera" and that guy with the gray hair was gonna come out and shake his hand.

He already had the money spent. Nine grand would go toward his debts. The other eight would go into the bank, maybe toward a down payment on a house in Staten Island or Jersey. Maureen had been begging him to move into a nicer place for years and he was sick of living in the city. He wanted to live in a place where he could own a car so he wouldn't have to take buses to the racetrack anymore.

Then the crowd started to jeer. Joey felt the Carvel and hot dogs collapsing in his stomach. He ran to the nearest TV monitor, afraid to see what he already knew. The food dropped another couple of inches when he saw the INQUIRY sign on the tote board.

When the eight horse had made that move to lead, Manzi had cut off the horses to his outside. Joey had seen this clearly, but he had blocked it out in his excitement. Now he prayed to God for a miracle. Joey was half Jewish, half Italian, and he didn't believe in religion, but he swore to God he would pray every day for the rest of his life if He would just put up the fucking OFFICIAL sign.

Sometimes the judges took five minutes or longer to decide whether a horse should be disqualified. Maybe tonight they were tired and wanted to go home because in less than a minute the tote board went blank and the revised order of finish was posted. The eight had been placed fourth.

Joey's horses had been disqualified before, but never for this much money and never when he needed the money this badly. He asked God what he had ever done to deserve this treatment and, as usual, he didn't get any answer.

Slowly, he walked toward the exit. He tried to tell himself that he wasn't any worse off than he'd been five minutes ago. But all he could think about was the damn INQUIRY sign and how nothing ever seemed to go right in his life. He was walking unsteadily. A few people bumped into him, saying "excuse me" or "sorry," but he didn't even seem to notice.

Leaving the grandstand, heading down the long ramp, Joey felt like he could lie down and sleep forever. But, typical of his luck, the bus had already filled and he had to stand the whole way back to Manhattan.

Two

"COME HERE," DAVID Sussman said, unzipping his pants.

Amy Lee put down the bottle of Bud Light she'd been drinking and started kissing David hard, pushing him back onto his desk.

A few nights a week for the past month or so, David and Amy stayed late at the R.L. Dwyer Advertising Agency on East Fifty-first Street, where they both worked, and had sex in David's office. Like the other flings he'd had during his marriage, David had figured that he and Amy would fool around a few times and then the affair would end painlessly. But David's previous affairs had been during business trips, far away from New York, and he hadn't anticipated all the complications of an office romance. He had to keep seeing Amy every day, smelling her perfume, and then there was the Chinese factor. David had always fantasized about having sex with an Asian woman and, although Amy was born and raised in Astoria, Queens, David still thought of her as "exotic." But lately his exotic image of Amy was wearing thin. He'd been feeling more and more guilty, thinking about his wife and ten-year-old daughter at home, and he'd decided that after tonight he'd definitely tell Amy the affair was over.

Although he went running three mornings a week and did sit-ups and crunches every night before bed, David still felt that he could stand to lose a few inches off of his waistline. He was six-one, had a long, gangly body, and dark curly hair. The summer before he'd left for college at Albany, he had gone to a plastic surgeon in his home town of Dix Hills, Long Island, and had excess cartilage removed from the tip of his nose. By the next summer, the nosejob had "caved in" and he thought he looked worse than before the operation. The surgeon couldn't guarantee that additional surgery would solve the problem so David continued to go through life obsessed with his appearance.

"Shit, it's after ten o'clock," David said, unconsciously sucking in his stomach as he pulled on his boxers.

"Come back down here," Amy said, grabbing his leg.

Wiggling free, David said, "Seriously, I have to get out of here. I told Leslie I'd be home by nine."

"Are we ever going to spend a whole night together?"

"Just get dressed," David said, finding his pants on the floor. He wanted to break the news to her now, but he wanted to make sure the words came out right. He'd always had trouble breaking up with women. He'd met his wife in college. Before that, he'd only had a couple serious girlfriends, and he never broke up with any of them. Either he would get dumped or he'd just start acting like an asshole until the girl finally got the message.

"My mother wants to meet you," Amy said.

"Your mother?"

"She asked me if I've been dating anybody lately."

"We're not *dating*," David said. He held up his hand,

displaying his gold wedding band. "See? This means I'm officially unavailable for dating."

"I told her I'd bring you home to Queens sometime."

"Very funny," David said, hoping Amy was joking. "Come on, let's get a move on."

"You're so sexy when you're nervous."

David looked down at Amy, still lying nude on the floor. He couldn't help noticing her flat stomach and the way no fat hung off of her twenty-six-year-old thighs.

"I think we should talk."

"I'm not in the mood to talk."

"How long has this been going on?"

"Fuck me again."

David loved it when Amy talked dirty. It usually gave him an instant hard-on, but this time he tried to hold back his excitement.

"I'm serious," David said, buttoning his shirt. "I've been thinking—maybe we shouldn't do this anymore."

It was a relief to finally get those words out. In a way, he felt as if just *saying* this negated the whole affair. It had never happened and now he had nothing to feel guilty about.

"I know you don't want to do that," Amy said.

"It isn't a matter of what I want."

"You see, that's what I don't understand about you. When you're working you're so confident. But as soon as the workday ends you're always talking about your wife—your wife this, your wife that. What about you? Are you going to spend your whole life being miserable just to make someone else happy?"

"Who ever said I was miserable?"

"What if you weren't married and there were two doors? I was behind one door and your wife was behind the other? Which ever door you opened, you'd be with that person for the rest of your life. Which door would you choose?"

Thinking that he probably wouldn't choose either door, David said, "I don't have time for this."

"I'm making it easy for you," Amy said in a breathy, Marilyn Monroe voice, spreading her legs farther apart. "My door's already opened."

"Put on your clothes," David said seriously.

He wound on his tie and started stuffing papers and folders he was bringing home into his briefcase. Amy didn't move off the floor.

"Come home with me."

"You know I can't do that."

"You mean *won't*."

"Whatever."

"Don't you want to fuck me in my bed?"

The dirty talk wasn't a turn on anymore.

"Just put on your clothes so I can lock up in here."

Amy was staring at David, her lips parted slightly.

"You know, the thought of you going back to your wife every night really upsets me," Amy said. "I think about us, how we were, and then I think about you with her and I can't help it—I get very angry at you."

"Look, it's over, all right?" David said. "I hate to put it like that, but it's the truth. We had some fun, but now we have to go on with our lives. That's just the way it is."

David looked away from Amy, toward the blind-covered window. He hoped she would just leave—end this thing nice and cleanly.

Amy said, "I thought you said you wanted to marry me."

"What?" David said, turning around suddenly. "How the hell did you get that idea?"

"You proposed to me last week."

David wondered if this could be true. It was possible he'd said *something* to Amy about marriage—maybe that night last week when he felt confused—but it definitely wasn't a marriage proposal and he definitely hadn't meant it.

"I never said I wanted to marry you," David said. "I said 'Wouldn't it be nice if we got married someday?' There's a big difference."

Amy glared at David. David felt like they were strangers on the street, looking at each other for the first time.

Amy said, "This is a joke, right? You're gaslighting me."

"Come on," David said, "let's try to be mature adults here—"

"Why would you lie to me like this?"

"I didn't lie to you," David said. "Maybe you *misheard* me."

"I know what I heard—I'm not crazy. You were standing right where you are. You said, 'Will you marry me someday?'"

"But I'm already married. Why would I say that?"

"That's a good question."

David looked away from Amy then he looked back at her and said, "Come on, get dressed. It's past eleven already."

"So let me get this straight," Amy said with a fake smile. "You don't want to marry me. I suppose you don't love me either. And what else did you tell me that night? Oh, that's right, that I'm 'the most beautiful, most exciting' woman you've ever met. I guess you didn't mean those things either."

"I never said any of that."

Amy had started to cry. David stood next to his

desk, looking down at her. She was still on the floor, naked, her head between her knees. David watched her for about a minute—first noticing how incredible she looked, then thinking about how crazy this situation was getting. Finally he said, "Come on, get dressed. This isn't doing either of us any good."

Amy looked up at David. Her eyes were red and her cheeks were lined with mascara.

"You meant all of this, didn't you?" she said. "You just want to pretend we never met."

David let out a deep breath then said, "I guess we can still say hi in the hallways."

Amy shook her head several times, then she stood up off the floor. She started to get dressed, pulling on her panties.

"I'm not desperate, you know," she said. "There are a lot of other guys I can be with right now, so you can just stop this high-on-your-horse, I'm-so-much-better-than-you routine because I couldn't care less."

"I'm sorry."

"Fuck your sorrys." She hooked on her bra. "You're not in control here, Mr. I Think I'm So Desirable, Mr. *Married* Man. What if I called your wife right now?"

Amy looked ugly—her eyes glazed, her nostrils flaring.

"Look, I said I was sorry."

"I can do it, you know. I can pick up the phone right now and tell your wife everything. I'll give her a blow-by-blow report of everything we've done together."

"I think you've made your point."

"861-4735."

David stared at Amy, hoping she would smile, but she didn't. His home number wasn't listed and he had no idea how she'd gotten it.

"Look, I think this is starting to get out of hand,"

David said. "It's late and we've both had long days—"

Buttoning up her blouse, Amy said, "Tell me that you love me."

"*What*?"

"I don't care what you say, I know you love me. If you're honest and admit that we're in love maybe I won't call your little wifey tomorrow."

"This is a joke, right? You're kidding."

"I want you to say I love you."

"I don't love you."

"Say it, David."

"I don't love you. I love my wife."

"So I guess you're ready to just flush your marriage down the toilet."

Amy had put on her skirt and now she was putting on bright red lipstick, looking at herself in a compact mirror.

"You better not call her."

"You better tell me you love me."

David grabbed Amy's arm. He realized he was squeezing too hard and let go.

"Please," he said, trying a different tack. "Look, if things were different—if I was younger, if I was single— then maybe it would be possible. But I made it clear, at least I *thought* I made it clear, that this wasn't going to be serious."

"I know what you said, and I know what I heard."

"Well you didn't hear right."

"Do you have any messages?"

"Messages?"

"...You want me to give Leslie. And Jessica. That's your daughter's name, isn't it?"

David couldn't remember ever telling Amy about his daughter. Amy tried to get by. David grabbed her arm again and held her.

"All right," he said. "If I say it, you swear you'll never call my wife?"

"I swear."

"Are you crossing your fingers?"

David let Amy go and she held up her hands. With his eyes closed, David said, "I love you."

"Who do you love?"

"For God's sake—"

"Say 'I love you, Amy.'"

"Jesus Chri—"

"I'll call your wife *and* daughter."

David noticed how the whites of Amy's eyes were visible all around her pupils.

"I love you, Amy."

"That's better. Now we're starting to make some progress."

*　*　*

When Amy left his office, David went right to the mini-refrigerator behind his desk and opened a bottle of Bud Light. He drank half the bottle without pausing for air. He still couldn't believe what had just happened. It was as if the past few weeks with Amy were a pleasant dream that suddenly turned into an all-out nightmare. He realized that the whole situation was mostly his fault. He had definitely led her on, made a few promises he couldn't keep, but how did he know she was going to snap?

Amy had only been with the agency for six months and David realized that he hardly knew her. She had once mentioned something about "seeing a shrink," which in itself didn't mean anything, but what if she had major psychological problems? All David knew about Amy was that she was from Astoria, that her parents had divorced when she was very young, and that she went to college at Parsons School of Design. Sometimes she spoke about past relationships, but always in vague terms. She would say, "This guy I went out with in college..." or "I was seeing this guy for a few weeks and so and so..." But she never mentioned any of her friends or relatives by name or talked about what she did in her spare time. David knew she lived in the Village, but he didn't know if it was the West Village or the East Village, not to mention what street she lived on.

David tried to remember why he had gotten involved with Amy in the first place and his mind came up blank. Just thinking about her gave him a sick empty feeling in the middle of his stomach.

No matter what, he decided, this was going to be the last affair he'd ever have. Affairs were too stressful and they weren't helping him the way they used to. They weren't enjoyable and they certainly weren't making him feel any younger.

David left his office, locked the door, and went down the quiet, carpeted hallway to the men's room. After he peed, he washed up and straightened his shirt collar and brushed off the arms of his sports jacket. As usual, the only thing he saw in the mirror was a bad nosejob. But then he moved closer to the glass and studied his forehead wrinkles and eye lines. New signs of middle age seemed to appear on his face every day. He was trying to cut down on drinking and junk food and he drank two ounces of wheatgrass juice every day during lunch. He took a wide assortment of vitamins, including super anti-oxidants such as CQ-10, cat's claw, and shark cartilage. He also took dosages of flaxseed oil and sprinkled bee pollen onto his cereal every morning. If these so-called aging remedies accomplished anything

David couldn't see the results. Sometimes he would stare at himself in the mirror and be astonished at how tired and leathery he looked. But nothing was worse than the surge of horror he would feel when he realized that in just three years he would turn forty. Forty had always seemed light years away, at the end of the universe, and it was incomprehensible to him that a man who felt so young could actually be on the brink of middle age.

Riding down in the elevator, David imagined what a disaster it would be if Amy called Leslie. Leslie had a very conservative attitude about marriage. Once, a friend of hers had discovered that her husband was cheating and Leslie said that the friend was "crazy for staying with him." When she saw movies or TV shows that dealt with adulterous men, she always called the men "bastards" or "pigs," and she'd once warned David flat-out that she would leave him if he ever cheated on her.

Suddenly, David felt dizzy. The walls of the elevator seemed to be closing in on him. He dropped to his knees and tried to catch his breath. When the doors opened in the lobby he got up slowly, then he stood outside the elevator, supporting himself against the marble wall. He'd had panic attacks on and off for most of his life, but lately they were getting worse. A minute or two passed and his strength returned. He wobbled through the lobby out to Second Avenue. The frigid wind stung his face and blew dust into his eyes. He walked with his chin tucked under his overcoat collar, his hand out to hail a taxi. As usual, a few cabs passed inexplicably, then one finally picked him up. Staring out at the dark, nearly deserted East Side streets and the dense clouds of sewer smoke billowing out of the manhole covers depressed David even more. All it would take was one phone call, and even if Amy didn't call Leslie tonight, she could call her some other time. David considered beating Amy to it, telling Leslie about the affair as soon as he got home. Or, better yet, he could warn Leslie that some crazy woman might be calling—someone whom he'd fired last week—and to ignore everything she said. She was psychotic, he'd tell her—right out of a mental institution. But Leslie was too smart for that. Just mentioning the subject of affairs would lead to endless probing and Leslie could always tell when David was lying.

David knew that Amy could ruin his entire life if she wanted to. He was Senior Marketing Manager and Amy was a graphic artist. Although they worked in completely different departments, technically, she was lower on the company totem pole. David didn't know whether this could constitute an harassment case or not, but he realized how moronic it was for him to even get into such a predicament. At least he'd been smart enough to use rubbers.

As the cab sped up Third Avenue, weaving in and out of traffic as if on the Indianapolis Speedway, David felt a click in his chest—*mitral valve prolapse syndrome*—the first signal of a new panic attack coming on. As his heart started to race, he drew his attention inward, focussing on his breathing. "In, out, in, out," he whispered. The technique worked and suddenly things didn't seem nearly as bad as they had a few seconds earlier.

"This is it, on the right," David said to the cab driver.

The cab pulled in front of David's building on East Seventy-ninth Street. Walking confidently into the wood-paneled lobby, David greeted Tom, his doorman, with a warm smile. It felt good to be in the protected domain of a luxury apartment building where nothing

could ever harm him. The elevator ride to the
nineteenth floor didn't cause him any discernible panic.
As usual, Leslie had left the living-room light on, and it
felt warm and relaxing to be in his apartment. In
addition to the living room and the three bedrooms—
David used the third bedroom as his office—there was a
dining room, two bathrooms, a terrace and an eat-in
kitchen. After drinking a glass of apple juice, he went
down the hallway to Jessica's room. He tip-toed up to
her bed where she was sleeping, then kissed her lightly
on the forehead. She stirred, rolling on to her side.

"I love you, daddy."

"I love you too, pumpkin. Sleep tight."

David washed up—trying not to notice the
deepening wrinkles under his eyes—and put on a clean
pair of underwear. The quiet in the apartment was
calming, refreshing. Leslie was sleeping soundly so
David decided not to wake her. He moved against her,
spooning her body, and wedging his face against the
back of her soft neck. It was comforting, smelling the
peach odor of her moisturizing cream and feeling his
heart beating steadily against her back. Only when he
thought about Amy Lee, and her crazed, staring eyes,
did he start to panic again.

Three

WALKING DOWN TENTH Avenue, still in a daze, Joey was unaware of the numbing cold or that his jacket was unzipped. He stopped, realizing that he was on the corner of Tenth and Fifty-first, three blocks past his building. He could hardly remember the bus ride or leaving the Port Authority Bus Terminal. He'd been so obsessed, thinking about that goddamn INQUIRY sign, that the last half hour seemed to have passed by in an instant.

Joey and Maureen DePino lived in a two-room walk-up apartment in a former Single Resident Occupancy building on Tenth Avenue and West Fifty-fourth Street. The rooms were as long and narrow as subway cars, with a tiny bathroom in the middle of the apartment opposite the front door. Maureen was constantly complaining about how the apartment was "too small" for two people, and she went on about the loud neighbors, the mildew in the shower, the crumbling brick wall, the missing tiles in the bathroom, the leaks in the ceiling, and the irregular heat and hot water. At the end of the room they called "the living room" there was a sink, a kitchen and a stove, but whenever Maureen cooked she complained that the smells attracted roaches and mice from the Korean deli downstairs. Because they couldn't afford new furniture, the apartment was decorated with furniture Maureen had bought in thrift shops and at flea markets—a futon couch, a big dresser, a square table, two chairs, and some old mirrors. Maureen said she was tired of living in a dump and she was always going on about how the building and the neighborhood weren't safe. Their apartment had been robbed twice and last year a young woman was raped in the building's vestibule.

Joey didn't think their apartment was a palace, but he didn't think it was as bad as Maureen made it out either. At least there were two separate rooms and who needed a kitchen? Anyway, he *liked* having a Korean deli in the building because it meant he could get a corned beef sandwich in the middle of the night without crossing a street.

Joey met Maureen seven years ago at The Raccoon Lodge on Amsterdam Avenue. Joey had a good job then, doing deliveries and installations for a lumber store on Broadway, and he was out on a Friday night, having drinks with a couple of old friends from Brooklyn. Maureen was sitting at the bar across from the pool table with a friend who was getting hit on by this other guy. One of Joey's friends told Joey that "the girl with the dark curly hair" was looking at him like he was "a piece of chop meat." Later, Maureen told Joey that she never noticed him until he came over and bought her a drink.

When Joey first looked at Maureen he didn't think there was any way in hell a girl like that would go for a guy like him. She was obviously a city girl, dressed in expensive-looking black clothes, and she was a hell of a lot better-looking than the girls he was used to going out with. The girls he knew, back in Brooklyn, had faces packed with zits, teased-up hair, skin-tight jeans, and they chewed on their gum like horses. But Maureen definitely looked like she had some class. She was sitting with her legs crossed, stirring a drink that had a piece of lime in it. It was always hard to tell a girl's weight when she was sitting down on a bar stool. Maureen didn't look fat, but she didn't look thin either. She was a chunky girl who probably needed to drop ten or twenty pounds, but she carried the extra weight in all the right places. In other words she was just Joey's type.

Joey didn't want to go over there just to get blown off, but his friends kept egging him on, telling him that the chick with the curly hair was "horny" and looked like she could "suck dick like a vacuum cleaner." Finally, after another beer, Joey made his move.

Right away, maybe two minutes into the conversation, Joey knew he was talking to the girl he'd marry someday. Later, Maureen would say she didn't believe him, that there was no way he could've known that soon, but Joey always swore it was the truth.

They stayed at the bar until closing time. Once or twice, Maureen got up to go the bathroom and Joey watched her walk away, liking what he saw. She had nice big hips and a thin waist. Their friends were gone and Joey and Maureen were both drunk. Joey walked Maureen back to her apartment, around the corner from the bar. In front of the building, Maureen asked Joey if he wanted to come up for a drink. He wound up staying at her apartment all weekend. Usually, Joey didn't like it when a girl spread her legs so fast, but Maureen was different. He used to tell his friends in Brooklyn that "there was no such thing as love," but that was before he met Maureen Byrne.

The only thing Joey worried about was that Maureen was too smart for him. He'd barely made it through high school and since then he'd been bouncing around from job to job. But Maureen was very bright—she did two years at Hunter College and she knew computers. She had a classy job too, as a legal secretary for some hot-shot law firm. Joey still didn't know why a smart city girl wanted to slum with a guy like him. He wondered if she just liked him for his body. He asked her about this one day and she just laughed, like it was some kind of joke.

Joey really felt like an idiot when he went out with Maureen and her preppy college friends. They'd sit around, talking about whatever, and Joey'd just sit there with nothing to say. But when Joey and Maureen were alone, Joey always felt comfortable, more comfortable than he'd ever felt around a woman, and he saved up two thousand dollars and went down to a jewelry store in Chinatown and bought Maureen the biggest rock he could afford.

After they got married, Joey warned Maureen that things were gonna be rough for a while. He said they'd probably live in a shitty apartment and they wouldn't be able to go on trips and they could forget about having kids for at least five years. Maureen said this would be no problem, that as long as she was with Joey she'd be happy. And they did have a good year or two where they hardly fought and they went out to dinner and a movie every Saturday night like a normal couple. Sometimes, in the summer, they went to Central Park or down to the South Street Seaport. Then she wanted everything too fast. She was always talking about how she was jealous of her friends who were living in nice apartments, and whose husbands were making big money. Joey never understood where Maureen got the idea they were gonna be rich someday. Yeah, he'd told her things were gonna be *better*, but by better he meant that maybe he'd land a job in a mailroom or managing a warehouse, and take in a few extra bucks a week. So things didn't work out those first few years, but he had a good job now, installing data and voice cabling for a computer networking company. So maybe five years till kids and a house was a pipedream. Maybe seven or ten would've been more like it, but Maureen wanted everything right away.

It didn't help when Maureen went to the doctor last year and found out she had a cyst on one of her ovaries. They had to cut her open and take the cyst out and now Maureen was afraid that if she didn't have kids soon she'd never be able to have them. "In four years I'm gonna be forty," she always said, like it was against the law to get pregnant when you were forty-one. And she never shut up about it either—kids this, kids that— didn't she have anything else to talk about? Joey always told her they couldn't afford kids now, but it was like he was talking to himself.

One time, Maureen said, "This wasn't what I expected my life to be like before I got married," and Joey said, "Well then you shouldn't've fuckin' married me." Then Maureen said, "I didn't know I was marrying a gambler."

Joey had a rule, never hit a woman, but when Maureen said things like that he felt like decking her. She always blamed all of their problems on gambling. So he went to the racetrack four or five nights a week— what, he wasn't allowed to have a hobby? Meanwhile, Maureen was the one turning into the fuckin' sorry sack. She never wanted to leave the house anymore or do anything. She just liked to sit on the couch every night, feeling sorry for herself. Joey once saw a TV show about women like Maureen who went through "the change of life" and started acting bitchy and depressed all the time when they got older. But that was when they got *a lot* older. Maureen was only thirty-six and she was acting like she was fifty.

*   *   *

When Joey opened the door to his apartment, gasping for air after the walk up three flights of stairs, Maureen was standing in the vestibule. She was wearing a pink terry cloth robe and no makeup. She had put on some extra weight the past few years, mainly on her stomach, hips and thighs. She was always going on about how she was fat and needed to lose fifty pounds, but Joey didn't mind it. He knew he was no John Travolta himself and he'd always felt sorry for guys who had to worry about leaving their skinny, good-looking wives at home.

"Where the hell have you been?" Maureen asked.

Joey didn't say a word. He walked past her, into the bedroom. The TV was on loud—Jay Leno interviewing somebody.

"I'm sick and tired of this crap, Joey. I want to know where you were tonight."

Joey took off his jacket and flung it on a chair, then sat on the bed and started taking off his sneakers.

"Bowling."

"Bowling? You're just gonna sit there and tell me you went bowling tonight?"

"That's right," Joey said, seeing the INQUIRY sign again and feeling a sharp twinge in his stomach.

"So how'd you do?"

"I lost," Joey said miserably.

"How much?"

"You mean what was my score?"

"No, I mean how much did you lose at the track?"

"The track?" Joey said, as if it was some remote part of the world. "What the hell are you talking about?"

"Stop playing games because I'm really not in the mood for it tonight."

"That makes two of us."

"You swore to me you'd stop gambling."

"Christ sake, Maureen, I have a headache," Joey said, pulling off his pants. He burped, smelling his own hot-dog breath. "I really don't feel like fighting with you now."

"If you're in a bowling league how come you never talk about the other players?"

"What do you mean? Guys from work."

"Guys from work? Which guys from work?"

Joey was staring at Jay Leno, wondering how that big ugly dork got a TV show.

"I'm talking to you."

"What do you want from me?" Joey said, suddenly yelling.

"I want you to stop lying to me! Where were you, at the OTB? At the Meadowlands? I can smell the smoke all over you."

"People smoke at the bowling alley."

"I'm not gonna take this anymore, Joey. Gambling away all our money is one thing, but at least you could be man enough not to lie to me all the time like I'm some kind of idiot!"

"Just leave me the hell alone, will ya?" Joey said, pushing past her. "I don't need this shit first thing when I walk into the house."

He went into the bathroom and sat down on the

bowl. He didn't have to go, but in a two-room apartment the bathroom was the only place he could get any real privacy. Usually, he'd bring in the *Racing Form* or the *Daily News*, but now he wasn't in any mood to think about gambling. How could he make another bet that could get him back seventeen thousand dollars? That kind of chance comes along once in a lifetime.

"Joey, come out of there right now."

"I'm taking a shit."

"Sure you are."

"Want me to open up the door so you can smell it?"

Joey heard Maureen make a frustrated, fed-up sound with the back of her throat. Seconds later, the bedroom door slammed.

After a few minutes, Joey calmed down and he felt bad for yelling at Maureen like that. He just wished she'd learn to leave him alone on nights he got the shit kicked out of him at the racetrack.

If all his debts were clean, if he had money in the bank, Joey swore to himself that he would never gamble again. Of course he had made this same promise to himself thousands of times before. After he was married, he went six months, maybe a year, without placing a single bet. But then football season started and the itch came back, stronger than ever. He tried to quit many other times—usually after taking big losses—and he'd always start again, sometimes the next day. Finally, he decided that there was no use trying to fight it. Some people liked to drink or do drugs or shop and his thing was betting. It was his fuel, his way of getting through the day. Without gambling he couldn't imagine living.

His brain was like a maze. Nine thousand dollars — the amount of money he figured he would need to clear all his debts—was at one end of the maze, and he worked backwards, exploring every possible way out. But he kept hitting dead ends. Finally, the only result of all his work was a throbbing headache. After swallowing three Extra-Strength Tylenols, he returned to the bowl, his chin resting on his palm. The only way he could possibly make nine thousand dollars was to somehow win it. The trouble was you need money to win money and he had no money in the bank. Tomorrow he'd get a paycheck, but it would only be about three hundred dollars and all of it would have to go toward February's rent. He needed at least a thousand dollars to make payments to Frank and Al and he had no idea where he was going to get it.

When Joey finally left the bathroom and went back into the bedroom, the light and the TV were off. Maureen was in bed and Joey hoped she had fallen asleep. He was still very aggravated and the Tylenols hadn't kicked in and he didn't want to take any more anger out on her.

"Joey."

"Yeah."

"I'm sorry. You're right. I shouldn't've started yelling at you like that. It was wrong."

"Forget about it," Joey said.

There was a short silence then Maureen said, "I mean you're my husband, right? So I guess that means I should trust you. If you said you went bowling tonight then you went bowling tonight and that's all there is to it."

Joey felt awful, but not awful enough to admit he'd lied. What would that do, except lead to another screaming match?

"Joey?"

"Yeah?"

"How do you feel?"

Now he understood why Maureen had apologized. It had nothing to do with trust.

Rubbing Joey's stomach, Maureen said, "You feel like..?"

"Nah," Joey said. "My fuckin' head's splittin' open."

Maureen's hand stopped moving. She kept it there for a few seconds, her fingers caught in Joey's stomach hair, then she yanked it away. She sat up.

"I need a straight answer, Joey."

"Not now."

"You never want to talk about it. It's never a good time."

"Jesus, Maureen."

"I just want to know the truth. I think you owe me that much."

"Why do you always do this to me?" Joey said. "Pick the worst time to bring up this shit? I try not to yell, I try to control myself—"

"A headache!" Maureen said. "Couldn't you come up with a more original excuse than that?"

"How the fuck are we..." He was going to say, "supposed to afford kids?" but he realized this would only lead to another argument about gambling. It was too late to fight and he knew *this* fight would last a long time. So instead he said, "I don't want to fuckin' talk about it," and turned on to his side.

After a minute or two, Maureen lay down, facing the other way.

Four

WHEN JOEY ARRIVED at work the next morning, he immediately opened the *Daily News* to the Vegas Line section. The Indiana Pacers were playing the Orlando Magic at home, and Joey didn't see how the Pacers could possibly not cover the eight-point spread. It had to be the best bet in the history of gambling.

To get even, Joey figured he needed to double six hundred dollars four times. He would make the Indiana bet with Frank, one of the bookies he was in debt to, by using a different name. Frank set a "pay-or-collect number" for all his clients. Once a gambler reached this number and it was a "collect" situation, he wouldn't take any more action. But there was a way around this rule. Joey had become friendly with one of Frank's runners, an old Jewish guy named Morty. When Joey reached his number—in his case a thousand dollars—Morty let him put bets in under different names. This was how he'd built up a four-thousand-dollar debt with Frank, by owing one thousand dollars under four different names, including his own. Morty didn't mind the arrangement because he trusted that Joey would eventually pay off all his debts. Morty worked off a percentage of all the money he collected and Joey was one of his steadiest clients.

After Indiana won—in his mind this was already a done deal—Joey would need to hit three other bets, double or nothing, to pay all his debts and bills. During lunch, he would go to the check cashing place on Broadway to cash his paycheck and then shoot over to the OTB on John Street. Maybe he could get lucky—hit a couple of races at Aqueduct this afternoon—and then he could make an even bigger bet on Indiana.

Joey was so absorbed in the Vegas Line, looking for other sure things, that he didn't hear his boss come up behind him.

"I told you to read the newspaper on your own time," Mark Conine said.

Mark was a short thin man with gray hair and a gray mustache. He was born in Romania—his family's original last name had been something with a lot of vowels that Joey couldn't pronounce—and raised in lower Manhattan. After college, in the early seventies, his parents had given him the start-up money for Tech Systems. Joey always hated Mark—not just because he was his boss, but because he was a wimp—a mamma and papa's boy who'd had everything handed to him on a silver platter. If he didn't have his company and his family to hide behind, he'd just be a slimy little nothing. All over the walls in his office were posters of naked women and race cars. He owned two Porsches and it sickened Joey whenever Mark opened his wallet and showed people pictures of the cars, like they were his kids. Joey always figured that Mark must have a very small dick. One day when they were pissing next to each other at the urinals, Joey looked over and sure enough it looked like somebody's pinky between Mark's thumb and index finger.

"Sorry," Joey said, closing the newspaper. "I was just checking something."

"Eh?" Mark said.

Mark often said "Eh?" to people, no matter how loud or clearly the person had spoken. At first, Joey thought that Mark might have some sort of hearing problem, but he finally caught on. It was all a power trip. By constantly saying "Eh?" Mark got people to repeat things, so he was in control of every conversation.

"I said I was just checking something," Joey said.

"Aren't you supposed to be somewhere now?"

"I'm working at Caldwell today."

"Eh?"

"I'm working at Caldwell today," Joey said louder.

"Why aren't you there now?"

"I was on my way," Joey said. "I just needed to stop by the office first to pick up some hubs."

"I've had this conversation with you before," Mark said, loud enough that the whole office could hear. "You need something, you call and have it delivered. You don't come here under any circumstances. You realize how much this costs the company? I can't bill for time you're not at the site."

"But you told me to come here," Joey said.

"Eh?"

"I said you told me to come here. The other day I called you and said we needed some hubs and wall plates and you told me to stop by the office today and pick them up."

"I meant on your lunch hour."

"You didn't tell me that."

"I shouldn't have to tell you. You know the rules here."

"All right," Joey said. He felt his temper rising again and he didn't want to do or say anything he might regret.

"What time did you leave work yesterday?"

"Yesterday?"

"Eh?"

"I said, 'Yesterday?'"

"Yeah, yesterday."

"The regular time," Joey said. "Five o'clock."

He was lying. He had really left work at about twenty to five to make the early bus to the Meadowlands and catch the last few simulcast races from California.

"How come Slav told me you left at four-thirty?"

"I don't know."

"Why would Slav lie?"

"I did not leave work at four-thirty yesterday," Joey said confidently. After all, this was true.

"That isn't the point," Mark said. "The point is things are building up. You're coming in late, you're leaving early, you're reading newspapers on the job. I've had it with this shit. No more second chances. One more wrong move and you're out of here."

After Mark turned and strutted away, Joey held up his middle finger and mouthed, "Fuck you." He often dreamt about the day that he'd win Lotto and go into Mark's office and tell him to go fuck himself. It would almost be as good as blowing him away, watching his brains splatter on the wall.

Joey wanted to find another job, but twenty-six thousand a year with benefits was the ceiling for a cable installer with less than three years experience. A couple of years ago, Joey was sick of bouncing around from job to job and he knew he had to find something steady to get Maureen off his back, so he answered an ad in the newspaper and learned how to install cable. It was a good career and he didn't mind the work, but Joey still wished he could find a job like the one he had after high school.

It was supposed to just be a summer job, but it turned out to be the best job Joey'd ever had, loading and unloading at a paint store on Utica Avenue in Brooklyn. He and a few other guys there started working a scam, taking paint off the trucks and selling it on the side to other distributors. The boss's books were so screwed up he never caught on. Meanwhile, Joey was making over forty thousand a year on top of his regular salary. Having all that loose cash around contributed to Joey's gambling problem. Whenever he lost a few hundred bucks at the track it didn't matter because he could always just steal more paint. Those were the days all right—he was single, living on his own in an apartment in Sheepshead Bay, and he had a shitload of money. On weekends, he and his friends would go to the track, or drive down to the casinos in Atlantic City. If he had a good night on the tables, Joey would buy himself a whore. One night, he and all his friends chipped in and had four black hookers—all with huge knockers—in their room all weekend long.

But Joey's dream life fell apart suddenly when Mario Cantello got out of prison. Cantello was a big-time wise guy in Brooklyn, connected to the Gambinos and John Gotti. One day, Joey and his friends got a message that Cantello wanted to see them at his house in Canarsie. Scared shitless, they thought their boss might have found out about the stealing and hired Cantello to take care of them. When they arrived at Cantello's house and saw him—a fat, bouncer-like guy in a white tank-top T-shirt with big arm muscles and a surveillance bracelet on his ankle—they thought their worst nightmare was coming true. But then Cantello surprised them, saying that he wanted them to keep stealing the paint—but to bring it to *him*. Apparently, now that the cops were watching his gambling and racketeering operations, he was looking for some new racket to go into, so he figured he'd go into the "honest" paint business. Cantello was willing to pay Joey and his friends for their efforts—not nearly as much as they were making when they were on their own, but a couple of hundred a week each. Joey's friends accepted Cantello's offer, but Joey decided it wasn't worth it. One day they wouldn't be able to steal the paint and Cantello would accuse them of selling it themselves. The parole officers didn't put that bracelet around Cantello's ankle because he cheated on his tax returns. Sure enough, two years later, Joey heard that his friend Timmy got both his legs broken and all his teeth knocked out with a hammer when Cantello thought he was stealing paint from him.

Joey took the subway to Caldwell & Caldwell, an accounting firm on Broadway off Fulton Street. The company was expanding on to another floor and Joey and three other guys from Tech Systems were installing the cabling for the new computer network. Joey was the only natural born citizen on the Tech cabling staff. The rest were Russian immigrants or illegal aliens. Mark hired them because they worked cheap and because they were over-qualified. In Russia, they were probably rocket scientists—here they ran cable for eleven dollars an hour. On staff were three Slavs, four Igors, two Vlads, two Sergeys, and one Boris. They seemed like nice enough people, but Joey couldn't stand working with them. It was like he had his mouth taped shut all day. They all talked to each other in Russian, laughing, while he was bored shitless. Joey wondered if maybe this was proof that there was a God after all. For stealing money all those years at the paint store God was punishing him—making him lay cable with a bunch of Russians. But this didn't make sense. His boss at the paint store was the biggest asshole in the world—he used to beat up his wife and kids all the time—and if there was a God, a reasonable God, he would have been glad that Joey was stealing from him. In fact, he would have left Cantello in jail to rot.

Everything in the world was definitely based only on luck. Some people won Lotto, some people walked down the street and air conditioners fell on their heads, and the rest of the world was somewhere in between. Unfortunately, Joey felt closer to the air conditioner guy than the Lotto guy.

At noon, the paychecks for Tech Systems employees were delivered to the Caldwell & Caldwell office. Like a track star exploding out of the starting blocks, Joey went to the check cashing place, then to the Off Track Betting office on John Street. Joey had been to every OTB in the city and, gifted with a sixth sense, he could always calculate which branch he was closest to at any given time.

The John Street branch was narrow and smokey— even though smoking in the branches was illegal—filled with the usual degenerates, but also some money-obsessed Wall Street types in suits and ties. Joey looked at the odds on the TV screen and was amazed to see that the horse he liked—the six—was twelve to one. They were making the three the favorite, a first time starter. Joey didn't bother buying a *Racing Form* or a program. He liked the six and he didn't want the past performances to talk him off it. He'd kill himself if he bet another horse and then the six won.

Joey had an OTB phone account where he could get track odds, but there were only five minutes to post and with the OTB tellers, city employees who worked slower than the workers at the Motor Vehicle Bureau, there was no chance of getting the money into his account in time to make a phone bet. So Joey figured the hell with OTB's five-percent surcharge—it would come out of the winnings anyway.

He was going to say "One hundred dollars to win on the six," but when he got to the window he was so sure that the six would destroy the rest of the field that he said, "Give me three hundred win on the six."

As the horses loaded into the starting gate, Joey's heart started to pound. His palms were sweaty and he started screaming things at the screen, "Come on, Jose!"..."Bring this horse home!"..."Come on with this six horse, Jose!" as if the six horse and Jose Martinez, the jockey, could hear him.

When the gate opened Joey's face was already bright red; his glassy eyes were wide open. The six horse broke on the lead, then dropped back until it was no longer on the screen. Joey prayed that the six would suddenly appear when the field reached the top of the stretch, but he didn't see the horse again until it crossed the finish line, more than ten lengths behind the rest of the field.

Down three hundred bucks, Joey wondered how the hell he was supposed to make a payment to Frank now.

*   *   *

David Sussman cringed, swallowing two ounces of wheatgrass juice. He wondered whether it was worth torturing himself. Everyone at health food stores and juice bars looked pale and sickly. Healthy-looking people ate at McDonald's.

Leaving the juice bar on the corner of Forty-fourth, David walked up Third Avenue among the hoards of business people taking their lunch hours. It was a beautiful day—freezing, but there was bright sunshine and hardly any wind. David felt particularly depressed and he wondered whether it had something to do with the wheatgrass. He'd read somewhere that it could have strange effects on people, causing upset stomachs, nausea, and fatigue. Maybe it could cause depression.

David had no other reason to be depressed. Amy hadn't come to his office this morning and he hoped that after a night's sleep she'd realized how ridiculous she was acting last night and she'd leave him alone from now on. Last month, David's base salary had been raised to ninety-six thousand a year and after his bonus he made about one-sixty. He had a great apartment, a beautiful wife and daughter. There was absolutely no reason why he shouldn't feel absolutely great about himself, and yet he still felt there was something missing. He knew that having affairs wasn't the answer, but he still felt as if his life didn't have the same pizazz as it used to. In ten years, he'd probably still be drinking wheatgrass juice and working in the same office. Then he'd be forty-seven, almost fifty.

As he waited for a light to change, David noticed a woman looking at him. She was young, blonde, and his first instinct was that she was checking him out. He stood up straighter, expanding his chest, then noticed that the woman wasn't looking at him, she was *staring* at him, with a slightly disgusted expression. Then he realized she was focussed on his hair and he wondered whether a bird had shit in it. At the next store window,

David stopped and looked at his reflection. He felt a weight drop in his stomach and he burped up the taste of wheatgrass. He was going bald. His hair, which used to be his best feature, was falling out. He couldn't remember the last time he'd examined his hairline but the balding seemed to have happened overnight. He'd heard about this before—men waking up one morning and finding all their hair on their pillows. Now other people passing by seemed to be staring at his head. He went to the nearest drugstore and bought a supply of Minoxidil. When he put the box down on the counter, the woman at the register didn't seem at all surprised that he was buying it, proof that the problem couldn't be all in his mind. He decided that he would join The Hair Club For Men. This was what happened when a man was about to hit forty. Before he knew it, he'd need one of those penile implant devices. He'd have to walk around all day with his erect dick wedged against his stomach.

At the office, David locked his door and rubbed some Minoxidil into the top of his forehead. Then he checked his afternoon calendar on his GroupWise program. He had meetings scheduled for one-thirty, three, three forty-five and four-fifteen. It seemed like all he ever did at his job was have meetings. Sometimes he wondered why the agency just didn't hire robots to come in every day and go to meetings for him. The one-thirty was a staff meeting, the worst kind. Everyone sat around, taking turns, talking about "office issues," everything from a multi-million-dollar account they were working on to how to fix a running toilet. After David spoke briefly about a billing problem he was having with Accounting, he zoned out again, thinking about his hair. Maybe the wheatgrass was making it fall out.

When the meeting ended, Andy Lawson, one of the junior marketing people, walked alongside David in the hallway.

Resting his open hand on David's back he said, "So how's it going with your Chinese babe?"

At first, David didn't know what Andy was talking about. He'd been obsessing so much about his hair that he'd forgotten all about Amy. Then he remembered, and he also remembered telling Andy about her a few weeks ago in the men's room, saying, "The only problem with fucking a Chinese chick is you're horny an hour later." He recalled how young and studly he had felt at the time, but now he realized how stupid he had been—so high-on-his-horse and proud of himself. He'd bragged to other people about Amy too, like a high school kid the first time he goes all the way. What the hell had he been thinking? Any of these people he'd mentioned Amy to could have called Leslie, or someone *they* told could have called her. David had never been in therapy, but he knew what a psychologist would be telling him now—that he had told people about the affair because he *wanted* Leslie to find out. But why would he want her to find out? He loved his family more than anything in the world and he didn't want to lose them.

"You mean, Amy?" David said, like he could barely remember her name. "I have no idea."

"What do you mean? You were all over that a couple weeks ago."

"Yeah, well I don't even see her much anymore," David said. "It wasn't such a big deal anyway."

"No big deal? The way you were talking about it it was. Everybody was real jealous of you too. A wife *and* a hot little thing like that on the side. Man..."

Andy was twenty-five, big and blond, from

Tallahassee, Florida. Like a lot of people in advertising, he had gone into the business after college because he wanted to get laid. Every big ad agency had so many young people making twenty-two thousand a year that the offices resembled post-graduate dormitories. Every day, at five o'clock, big groups of R.L. Dwyer people "took over" one of the nearby bars on Second Avenue. On most week days they would stay at the bar drinking until midnight or one a.m., but on Thursdays, and especially Fridays, the pack would leave the first spot at around midnight, migrating to bars and clubs on the Upper East Side, not going home until two or three a.m. It was no mystery why people who stayed in the advertising business their whole lives turned into full-fledged alcoholics. When he first joined the agency after college, David used to drink every night, but when he hit thirty he'd stopped drinking the hard stuff. Now he only had an occasional Bud Light. In the old days, he probably would have been acting just like Andy, trying to get "thirty-something guy" in the office to talk about his drinking or sexual exploits, and the thirty-something guy, getting defensive would have said, like him, "Who's everybody?"

"I don't know," Andy said. "Just everybody."

"I didn't realize it was such a fast-breaking news item."

Andy smiled, looking confused. There were dark circles under his bloodshot eyes, as if he had a hangover.

"Come on, man," Andy said. "You should be proud of yourself, scoring with a babe like that."

"I said it was no big deal," David said, getting upset.

"Hey, I'm sorry, man," Andy drawled. "I didn't mean anything by it."

They were in the corridor, heading toward the Third

Avenue side of the office where the Marketing Department was. A couple of young girls—a year or two out of college—walked by, staring at David as they passed. Thinking about his hair again, David got even angrier. He said, "You know it's about time you grew up. You're what, twenty-five now? You should be thinking about your future, about what you're going to do after you hit thirty. You want to wind up an alcoholic in twenty years, on the liver transplant list? I'm not joking so you can just wipe that stupid smile off your face. Do you realize I'm one of your supervisors at this job? That means I play a role—a very significant role in determining your future. What if I gave you a shitty-fucking recommendation when you left this job? You realize how incestuous the advertising business is? No agency would ever hire you. They can always get some twenty-one-year-old guy who hasn't burnt his brains out yet to work for half of what it would cost to hire you. So before you come up to me, with your smug attitude, telling me what I should be 'proud' of, I think you should remember who you're talking to. If you don't show some respect around here you're going to wind up on skid row, pounding the pavement faster than you think."

They had stopped walking and were standing in the open part of the office. The secretaries were peering out of their cubicles and people passing by had stopped to see what all the commotion was about.

"I'm sorry, man," Andy said. "I mean I...I..."

David stormed away into his office, slamming the door so hard the whole wall shook. It felt good for a few minutes, like a star walking off stage after a bravura performance, but then David realized how crazy he must have sounded. Everyone probably thought he was losing his mind, having a nervous breakdown, or the people who could put two and two together would assume it had something to do with Amy Lee. After the President of the company, Robert Dwyer III, found out about his scandalous behavior—screwing a fellow employee in the workplace and screaming at another employee like a madman—David realized that he could be pounding the pavement a lot sooner than Andy Lawson.

Eric Henrickson opened the door to David's office. As Associate Marketing Manager, Eric shared many of David's clients and, outside of the office, Eric was one of David's few work friends. Occasionally, Eric and his fiancée, and David and Leslie, had gone out to dinner and movies.

"So what happened out there?" Eric asked.

He was short, stocky and wore wire-rimmed glasses. He always reminded David of a guy who could have been an accountant.

"Oh, nothing," David said, sitting at his desk, unconsciously touching his hairline. "I've just had a pretty shitty week."

"Trouble on the home front?"

"No, everything's fine. It's just...I don't know what it is. But don't worry, I'm not losing it. That's all I need—more rumors about me going around this place."

"This doesn't, by chance, have anything to do with that woman from Creative, does it? What's her name again?"

"Amy Lee, and no it doesn't," David said adamantly.

"All right. Sorry. I was just trying to help."

"Well, I don't need your fucking help."

David had never yelled at Eric before and he wondered if maybe he *was* having some sort of breakdown.

"Okay," Eric said. "Forget I asked. But, you know, maybe it's time for a little vacation."

David remembered his last vacation—going to North Miami Beach to visit Leslie's parents. That's what they did every December—a week with a bunch of geriatric Holocaust survivors scrutinizing him every day to make sure he was wearing the condominium arm bracelet to the health club. As if to get back at the Nazis they had to make life hell for everyone else. And they'd keep going to condo-mondo land until Leslie's parents eventually croaked. Then he'd be how old, sixty? Sixty-five?

"I'm sorry," David said. "I didn't mean to take anything out on you. Maybe it does have something to do with Amy. Last night she flipped out on me."

"What do you mean 'flipped out?'"

"I mean she lost it—totally. She got all angry and possessive. She threatened to call Leslie and Jessica."

"You're shitting me."

"Believe me, there was nothing funny about it."

"So what did you do?"

"What could I do? Hopefully she cooled off because I haven't seen her all day. But I'm telling you, I think the whole thing really shook me up. It made me think about what I've been like the past few weeks. I've really been a major league asshole. I've fooled around before, but never anything like this. This wasn't me—going around bragging every day about my sexual conquests like some Latin lover. It's like something got into me— something I couldn't control. Fuck, I don't know what I'm trying to say."

"So you got a little carried away," Eric said. "It happens to the best of us."

"What do you know?" David said.

"I cheated on a girlfriend once," Eric said. "It's not a good feeling."

"Yeah, well cheating on your wife is a little bit different," David said. "I can't just break up with her and start seeing somebody else. Fuck, we've been married fifteen years, together for eighteen. I have a daughter too and I could lose it all, just like that."

"I don't understand why she'd flip out like that," Eric said. "I mean if she didn't have a reason."

"What do you mean?"

"I mean you didn't lead her on, did you? Promise her anything?"

Thinking about how he'd asked Amy to marry him, David said, "You think I'm crazy?"

"Something must've set her off," Eric said.

"Have you ever seen patients in a mental hospital, the way you can see the whites around their eyes and they hardly ever blink? Well, that's the way she looked. And the way she spoke—in an even, threatening tone like she was from another planet."

"So what are you gonna do?"

"I have no idea. Hopefully it's all over with now anyway. I haven't seen her all morning so maybe she finally got the message. But do me a favor—don't talk to anybody else about this, all right? I feel like an idiot for the way I've been bragging about her around here like I'm in a locker room. I don't want her to overhear people talking about it and getting any more ideas."

"*No problema*," Eric said.

"But there's still one thing I don't understand," David said. "She knew my home phone number and my daughter's name. I have no idea how she found those things out."

"I guess that's my fault," Eric said, looking down.

"She stopped me in the hallway the other day. I was rushing out, not really thinking. She said she had to call you about something important."

"*You* told her?"

"I really wasn't thinking."

"Why did you mention Jessica?"

"She said she'd met her once before and she'd be embarrassed if Jessica answered the phone and she didn't remember her name."

"But why..." David was about to blow up again, but realized how little it would accomplish. The Amy thing was over and done with, if that was really what was upsetting him so much, and there was no use blaming Eric.

For the rest of the afternoon, David tried to keep himself busy with his work. At four o'clock, he got on a conference call with a client and R.L. Dwyer's rep at CNN, and when he got off he discovered it was after six. He'd told Leslie he'd be home early tonight for dinner and he wanted to call her to say he was on his way home. He was on the phone with Leslie when Amy appeared in his office. She was wearing a short black skirt—she always wore short skirts to work, but this one was shorter than usual, barely covering her thighs—and a white, silk blouse. She had on her usual dark red lipstick and her straight black hair was parted to the side. With the same vacant expression she'd had last night, she just stood by the door, staring at David.

Feeling another panic attack coming on, David tried not to show it. He kept smiling, listening as Leslie told him to stop at the gourmet food store around the corner from their apartment building, to pick up a half pound of gaeta olives.

"All right, sweetheart. I love you very, very much."

The "I love you" and especially the "very, very much," were meant more for Amy than for Leslie. When David hung up he said, "What the hell are you doing here?"

"What do you mean?" Amy said. "I thought we had a date."

"I think I made myself very clear yesterday … last night. I don't want to cause any more tension between us."

Now Amy smiled—a restrained smile that seemed almost threatening—and said, "That's the same thing I want—no more tension."

She strutted toward David's desk, like she might start to do a strip tease. Several times she'd stripped for David, using his desk as a stage. Thinking about what a jerk he'd been, sticking rolled-up dollar bills into her panties, gave David a sharp pain in his stomach. The twinge of excitement growing in his balls made him even more upset.

"Amy—"

"What's wrong? I thought you told me last night that you loved me."

"You forced me to say that."

"All I remember is that you said it."

Amy stopped in front of David's desk. She started to take off her blouse.

"How about a nice little fuck? Right here on the desk."

David caught himself imagining what that would be like. He felt another, stronger twinge—his penis was pressing against the inside of his leg—and he said, "I don't understand what the hell is wrong with you? Do you have some sort of problem or something? Because if you do that's okay, I understand that. But what you have to understand, okay, is that I'm a married man. A happily married man. It might be difficult for you, I know. You might feel rejected or feel that I'm deserting you. You told me your parents were divorced, right? Well, maybe that has something to do with this. I know how difficult that can be because my parents are divorced too. Maybe you blame your father—maybe you think all the father figures in your life are deserting you. Look, I'm not a shrink, and I don't really want to get inside your head. That wouldn't be any of my business. What I'm trying to say is it's okay. If I did anything to upset you I honestly didn't mean it."

Amy yawned.

"I was afraid you were going to play hard to get again," she said. "Well, I guess we'll just have to go through all the same bullshit."

"'Bullshit?'" David said.

"You told me that you love me and that you want to marry me," Amy said. "I think you're just having a hard time admitting it to yourself. I don't want to get inside your head—'that really wouldn't be any of my business,'" she said mockingly, "but a lot of guys have fear-of-commitment problems. And since you're married it must be doubly difficult for you."

"You're crazy," David said. Then, realizing this might incite her further, he said, "I mean you're *acting* crazy. I honestly think you should see someone. If it's your career you're worried about, I'm sure you can handle it discreetly. No one has to know you're going on leave for psychiatric problems."

"Maybe you should go to Word Perfect on your computer now," Amy said, "to the G-drive."

"And why should I do that?"

"You'll find out."

David looked at Amy, wondering if it was stupid of

him to try to analyze her.

"I don't have time for these games," David said. "I have to go home to have dinner with my family."

"You may not have a family if you leave here without doing what I tell you to do."

"Are you threatening me?" David said, realizing that the question was rhetorical and that there was nothing he could do about it anyway. What would he do, call the cops?

"You were the one who wanted to play hard to get," Amy said.

Figuring it might be the only way to get out of here quickly, David turned around in his swivel chair and brought up Word Perfect.

"What drive?"

"G," Amy said. "As in G-String."

David clicked on the G-drive.

Amy said, "Now go to users—file name prissy."

"What?"

"Prissy." She spelled it. "Because that's how your wife seemed to me today. Very prissy."

David turned around in his chair.

"What the hell are you talking about?"

"Click and you'll see."

"Prissy" was a bitmap image file and after David clicked with the mouse it took several seconds for the image to appear. First green and blue and gray colors appeared, followed by the faint outline of two people.

"So what is this supposed to be?" David said.

As the image came in clearer David saw bright lights, fast-food restaurant marquees in the background, and then he realized that the two people were women. But his panic didn't really set in until he saw who the women were.

"When the fuck was this taken?"

It was Leslie and her friend Maureen, sitting at a table in a restaurant or cafeteria. It was daytime and Leslie had on a light blue cashmere sweater and Maureen was wearing a brown jacket.

"Answer me," David said. "Where was this taken?"

"Calm down," Amy said. "I already heard about your outburst this afternoon. You don't want word to get around the office that *you're* crazy."

David looked back at the screen. Leslie and Maureen both had very serious expressions. Plastic trays filled with salad rested on the table between them.

"I'm asking you one more time," David said.

"All right, if you must know, it's the Manhattan Mall."

Now he recognized the fast-food counters in the background—the wide windows facing Sixth Avenue.

"When the hell was it taken?"

"This afternoon. I went to one of those one-hour photo places and had it developed, then I scanned it into the network."

"You didn't talk to her, did you?"

"No, of course not, but I could have if I wanted to. As you can see, I was very close to them."

It looked as if the picture had been taken from about twenty feet away.

"Did they see you?"

"No. Not while I was taking the picture I mean. But your wife definitely saw me afterwards. You see, we went shopping together."

"*What?*"

"I have to admit, David, your wife is very attractive, but she's a little past her prime, don't you think? You go more for the athletic type with the slim thighs and the abs of steel—like *moi*. And her attitude *has* to go. Where did a woman from the Bronx get the idea that she's God's gift?"

"How do you know she's from the Bronx?"

"I told you—we went shopping together. After she split off with her friend I followed her to Macy's. I don't know why you let that woman have free reign with your credit cards. It's a good thing I talked her out of buying that Donna Karan dress. I told her it didn't flatter her figure, but the truth is she looked old in it."

"I thought you didn't talk to her."

"I didn't tell her who I was. She thought I was a stranger helping her pick out a dress. It's not so uncommon, you know."

"Why?" David said. "And how did you know where to find them?"

"You're just lucky I didn't play this for her."

Amy opened her purse and took out a mini-cassette recorder. She pressed the PLAY button.

"*I love you, Amy.*"

"Give me that tape."

"Shh," Amy said, gesturing with her head toward the door. "People are still in the office."

"I said give it to me right now."

David was standing up, reaching over his desk.

"All right," Amy said. She popped out the cassette and handed it to him. "But it won't do you any good. I have copies at home and I also have other recordings— like the times you called out my name when you were fucking me."

David unwound the tape and ripped it apart. Then he put the cassette on his desk and crushed it with his paperweight.

"Be at my place tonight at nine o'clock," Amy said.

"My address is also on the G-drive—file name 'horny.' Be there on time or Little Miss Prissy hears my whole tape collection."

"What if I don't come?" David said.

"You will," Amy said smiling again. "You haven't disappointed me so far."

Five

MAUREEN WAS READY to give Joey an ultimatum—either he goes to Gamblers Anonymous or they get a divorce.

Having lunch with her best friend Leslie had given her a lot of confidence. Leslie and Maureen had grown up together in the same building at the Co-op City apartment complex in the Bronx, but Maureen always felt that they were more like sisters. After Maureen's mother died, her father fell into a deep depression. A few years later he lost his job selling insurance at State Farm and he started drinking heavily. It was Maureen's first year of high school and every day she'd come home and her father would be passed out on the couch. She tried to get help for him—she called her father's brother, her uncle, who was a doctor in Manhattan, but he didn't want to get involved. Meanwhile, her father was getting nastier. One day she came home from a school with a guy and her father called her a "slut" and a "whore" right in front of him. Finally, Maureen couldn't take it anymore and she started spending most of her time at Leslie's apartment.

Maureen always thought of Alan and Elaine Schlossberg as her "real parents". One year they took Leslie and

Maureen on a vacation to Florida and one summer
Maureen spent an entire month with Leslie's family at a
bungalow colony in the Catskills. Maureen celebrated
Jewish holidays with the Schlossbergs, but to make
Maureen feel comfortable Elaine Schlossberg always
cooked Christmas and Easter dinners.

Although Leslie was by far Maureen's closest friend,
Maureen had always secretly envied her. Leslie had a
perfect small face, beautiful hair, a great thin body, and
to top it off she was a great artist. In high school, the art
teachers used to hang her pictures in the hallways and
every day people would stop and stare at them, raving
about Leslie's talent. Maureen couldn't imagine what it
would feel like to be Leslie, to never know what it was
like to be unhappy.

When Leslie went away to college at Albany,
Maureen felt abandoned. She had been accepted to
Hunter College, but she didn't want to stay in her
apartment with her father. They hardly spoke anymore
and his drinking was getting even worse. He fought
with strangers on the street and one day he hit Maureen
so hard she had a black-and-blue mark under her eye
for two weeks. That was the final straw. Maureen
moved to Manhattan and lived with a roommate on the
West Side, going to Hunter during the day and doing
temp work as a data processor at night. She took
political science courses and was thinking about going
to law school someday. But after two years of college,
she couldn't stand the financial pressure anymore, so
she dropped out of school to work full-time as a legal
secretary.

Maureen had dated throughout high school and
college, but she had never had a steady boyfriend.
Maureen always thought that she carried too much

baggage with her family problems and that it scared guys off. In Manhattan, Maureen's luck with men didn't improve. She found it harder and harder to meet nice guys, which surprised her because she felt like she was getting better looking with age. She had grown her hair out and had lost weight and she had learned how to wear makeup. But when she went out to bars with friends the good-looking guys always ignored her and most of the time nobody talked to her at all.

When Leslie came back from college and moved in with her boyfriend David, Maureen hoped her own love life would improve. Maureen thought David was smart and very cute—the perfect man for the perfect woman. Maureen was often "the third wheel" on Leslie and David's dates, going to bars and restaurants and movies with them. A few times, David set Maureen up with friends of his from college. Maureen dated one of his friends for a couple of months, but it didn't work out.

Ten lonely years passed by and Maureen was still single. Then, one night at a bar on the West Side, around the corner from her apartment, Maureen met Joey DePino. He was a sweet, funny, working-class guy from Brooklyn. Maureen liked that he was half Jewish, half Italian—it somehow reminded her of her own upbringing. She also liked that she was better-looking than him and that he was uneducated. When she was out with Joey, Maureen felt good about herself.

If Maureen knew anything about gambling addiction before she met Joey, there was no way she would have married him. On their dates Joey talked about how he loved gambling and how he'd been going to the racetrack since his father started taking him when he was a kid. A couple of times, Maureen even went with Joey to the Meadowlands in New Jersey, and once they went to Atlantic City for a weekend. Maureen thought it was unusual the way Joey would get excited just *talking* about gambling, and she had a feeling he was betting more money on the races than he was telling her. But Maureen figured that gambling was just "a guy thing," like watching football on Sundays or playing golf, and that it would eventually fit into their lives.

For the first year of their marriage, Joey hardly gambled at all, but then he started going to the racetrack again. At first it was only on Saturdays, but before Maureen knew it he was going to the track three or four days a week. When he was home, life wasn't any better. If Joey wasn't betting on sports on TV, he always seemed angry and distracted. Maureen felt like she couldn't have a normal conversation with him anymore. Whenever she tried to talk to him about her problems, he would get angry and snap at her. Maureen was quickly realizing that gambling was a disease, just like drinking, and the whole situation was dredging up bad memories.

Gradually, Maureen started to put on weight. She tried dieting, but her problems with Joey kept driving her to food. She was five-six and weighed 185 pounds. She began hating herself for the way she looked and she hated Joey for making her this way. Maureen felt trapped—by Joey, by her apartment and by her job. She'd been working for the same group of ambulance-chasing lawyers for the past nine years. She knew she was smart enough to work at any job she wanted—sometimes she felt like she could do the lawyers' jobs better than *they* could—but that would mean going back to school and finishing college and how could she do that the way Joey was gambling all the time? If it weren't for her paying the bulk of the rent and the bills these past few years, Maureen didn't know what might have happened to them.

Maureen was getting sick of the whole situation and now time was running out. If she didn't have children soon she was afraid she'd never be able to have a family. Maureen's biggest nightmare of growing old, living alone with Joey in the same rundown apartment, seemed like it was becoming a reality.

* * *

"It's time to think about yourself," Leslie had told Maureen. They were sitting at a table in the back of the Manhattan Mall Food Court. "You have to ask yourself, 'Is this what I really want in my life right now? Is this where I want to be?'"

"Easy for you to say," Maureen said.

Maureen had always thought that Leslie and David had the ideal marriage. If her marriage were half as good as Leslie's she wouldn't have complained.

"You can have whatever you want," Leslie said, "but it all starts with yourself. If you think you don't deserve the good things in life, if you think you were meant to be miserable and depressed, then that's the way you'll be. Believe me, if you could see what I see you'd know exactly what to do. I see a vibrant, young, attractive woman, married to an inconsiderate, self-centered, sick man. Because he *is* sick, Maureen. I hope you're finally starting to realize that."

Leslie was always giving Maureen pep talks, telling her to get rid of Joey, but today it had finally sunk in. Maureen had never believed in the idea of divorce, but she didn't think she deserved to suffer either.

When Joey came home, Maureen was waiting by the

door, ready for a confrontation.

"Not again with this shit," Joey said. "I'm really not in the mood."

"I have something important I want to talk to you about," Maureen said.

"You hard of hearing?" Joey said. He went into the kitchen. He tossed his Giants jacket on a chair and opened the refrigerator. "Isn't there ever anything to eat in this fucking apartment?"

Maureen could tell that something was seriously wrong with Joey. Fearing that he had gambled away the rent money, she said, "What's wrong?"

"The pickles," Joey said rummaging in the back of the fridge. "What the fuck happened to the pickles?"

"I threw them away the other day."

"You did *what?*"

"They were old."

"You just bought them a couple of weeks ago."

"It was a couple of months ago."

"So? Pickles don't go bad."

"I'll get you new pickles."

"Unbelievable. No fucking food in the house and the food we do have you throw away."

"What's wrong, Joey?"

"I'm starving, that's what's wrong. Isn't there anything to eat in this goddamn house?"

"Did you gamble away the rent money?"

Joey slammed the refrigerator door.

"I asked you a question," Maureen said, "and it has to do with what I wanted to talk to you about. You know, I'm a vibrant, attractive woman and I deserve better than this."

"What the hell are you talking about?"

Maureen was confused. She tried to remember the

other things Leslie had told her to say and her mind was blank. She said, "You were gambling today. You lost our rent money and I can't take it anymore. This isn't what I want. I deserve better than this."

"I wasn't gambling," Joey said.

"Then what happened?"

"All right, if you really want to know, I got fired."

"Fired?"

"Is there an echo in here? And I don't want to talk about it. I just want to get some food and sit down in front of the TV and forget all about it."

Following Joey into the bedroom, Maureen said, "What happened?"

"Was I just talking to myself?"

"I have a right to know what happened."

"Nothing happened. That fucking pencil-neck prick had a bone up his ass, that's all. Cocksucker."

"He wouldn't've fired you for no reason."

"Well, he did. He's always had it in for me, since the day I got there. It's because I'm not an immigrant. He likes people who don't talk back to him."

"What happened?"

"I was late from lunch. No big deal—a few minutes. We had some words—that was it."

"He must've had some other reason."

"I'm telling you, that was it. The little scumbag was out to get me. I wasn't even working at the office. I was at a site on Broadway and he calls there at one-thirty to see where I am. Can you believe that shit? He doesn't check up on anybody else. It's like he wants to put a fucking leash around my neck. Fuckin' prick."

"Where were you?"

"What?"

"During lunch."

"What do you mean?"

"Why were you late getting back?"

Joey hesitated.

"I was at a pizza place, having a couple of slices. I had the *Daily News*. I guess I lost track of time."

Maureen stared at Joey, trying to figure out if he was lying.

"It's the truth, I swear to fucking God. Does this face look like it's lying to you?"

The buzzer sounded, someone calling from the intercom in the vestibule. Joey, glad to have the interruption, rushed to answer it.

"Leave it," Maureen called behind him. "It's probably some kids playing games again."

"It could be the super," Joey said, "forgetting his key."

Maureen heard Joey talking to someone on the intercom. She was wondering how she would give Joey the ultimatum tonight, after he'd already gotten such bad news. Joey came back into the bedroom, wearing his filthy Giants jacket she'd been begging him to throw away, and said, "Gotta go. I'll be back in a while."

"Where are you going?"

"Out."

"Out where?"

The door slammed.

Maureen didn't believe that Joey was at a pizza place this afternoon. He was gambling again, like he was going to gamble now, and she didn't want to know anything about it. She went into the living room and turned on the TV to The Food Channel. It was funny—she hadn't spoken to her father in thirteen years and she didn't even know if he was dead or alive, but lately she couldn't stop thinking about him.

* * *

In the six years that he had been putting in bets with Morty, Morty had only come to Joey's apartment one time—to pay him the three grand he'd won on a baseball bet. Somehow Joey knew that Morty wasn't here tonight to make a payoff, but he was still glad to hear his voice on the intercom. He wasn't in the mood to explain to Maureen how he'd been fired from his job because he was in the OTB until three o'clock trying to chase his money.

Morty, an old, hunched-over Jewish man, was standing in front of the building with a very serious expression. Joey decided to play it cool, like nothing was wrong.

"Morty, long time no see," he said. "Funny you should come by, I was just gonna call in a bet on Indiana. I fuckin' love Indy tonight."

"We gotta talk," Morty said grimly.

"All right," Joey said. "Hey, you know me, I love talking. Wait till I tell you what happened to me at the Meadows last night. You won't believe it."

"This is serious," Morty said. "You're...we're in a hell of a lot of trouble."

Joey's mind was spinning, trying to figure out what Morty meant by "a hell of a lot of trouble," but he managed to maintain his jokey attitude.

"Hey, my middle name's trouble. By the way," Joey looked at his watch, "shouldn't you be home taking bets now?"

Morty was always by his phone between six and seven-thirty and it was past six.

"Frank shut me down."

"What?" Joey said. He was terrified that he might not be able to put in his Indiana bet tonight. "Why? What happened?"

"Is there someplace we can go to discuss this," Morty

said, "a diner or something? I'm freezing my *tuchas* off out here."

Joey's mother had used a lot of Yiddish words, but she had been dead for nineteen years and Joey had forgotten the words just like he had forgotten most things about her. He thought that *tuchas* meant ass, but he knew that Morty wasn't in a joking around mood so he decided to keep his mouth shut.

They walked to a diner on Ninth Avenue, Morty refusing to tell Joey what was going on until they were sitting down. They sat at a booth in the back, near the bathroom. Mirrors covered the walls and the booths were made of pink vinyl. The whole place had a strong ammonia odor, like the bathroom in a Greyhound Bus. Without looking at the menus, Joey ordered a cup of coffee and Morty ordered a cup of tea and a Jello with whipped cream.

"So," Joey said, "what the hell's going on?"

"We're up shit's creek," Morty said, "that's what's going on. Frank found out."

"Found out?"

"About you...us...how I've been letting you bet under different names."

Wondering again how he was going to get in that Indiana bet, Joey said, "Shit."

Morty said, "He called me yesterday—wanted to know who 'Tony', 'Nick', and 'Vinnie' were. So what was I gonna say? I tried to cover for you, say they were guys I knew from downtown. But me and Frank go way back and he knows when I'm bullshitting him. He said to me, 'Tell me the truth, Morty.' So I told him."

"What did he say?"

"He flipped. He said, 'How could you let that fucking degenerate Joey DePino keep betting?' I tried to tell him that it's no big deal, that you always pay, but he was in a shitty mood. I heard his girlfriend dumped him last week and he's taking it out on everyone. That's when he said he's shutting me down. You know how long I've been working for him? Thirty-seven years come this May—twenty-two for his father, fifteen for him. And I've always been the most honest runner he has. Other guys skim, rob him blind, but not me. I've never taken a cent from that man."

"I'm really sorry," Joey said.

"Why? It's not your fault. He's the one who doesn't show any respect. It makes a man think about what he's been working for all these years. I have a daughter, two beautiful granddaughters, but I don't have any money put away. I have some stock, CDs, a few mutual funds, but it's *bubkis* compared to most men my age. You know how old I am? Come on, take a wild guess."

"Seventy-three."

"You're right. How the hell did you know that?"

"It was your birthday last week."

"See? Even my memory's starting to go. At least I still know the difference between my telephone and my toothbrush."

The waitress came with the coffee, tea, and the Jello. When she was gone Joey said, "So what do we do about this?"

After taking a sip of tea Morty said, "We relax, we don't get excited. I told Frank you'd come up with two grand by tomorrow, just to show you're good for it. I'm sure once you make that payment he'll consolidate your debt, put it all under one name, and when it's paid off you can start betting again."

"I can't afford two thousand."

Morty stared at Joey. His eyes suddenly seemed

bigger and darker.

"How much can you afford?"

Joey made the zero sign with his index finger and thumb.

Morty stared at Joey, not blinking at all. He said, "Look, I can tell Frank eighteen hundred. I'm sure I can get him to take that."

"I don't got eighteen hundred bucks," Joey said.

Now Morty took a deep breath, letting the air out slow. He said, "What are you telling me? I put my ass on the line for you because you told me you were good for this money."

"I know, and I appreciate that."

"I don't care how you get the money, but get it. Take money out of the bank, sell something."

"I don't got money in the bank and I have nothing to sell."

Morty took another long breath. Joey saw the muscles moving around his mouth and heard his denture plate grinding. Morty said, "How much *can* you afford?"

"Zilch," Joey said seriously. "I got canned at my job today."

Morty stared at Joey, letting this soak in, then he started talking in Yiddish, so fast that Joey couldn't make out what he was saying. He only recognized one word, "*mishugass*," which he thought meant bullshit.

"So what do I do now?" Morty said speaking English again. "I don't think you understand how angry Frank is. I didn't want to scare you before, but he said he might want to set an example with you. When are you going to take it seriously, when you're sinking in the East River wearing a pair of cement shoes? He doesn't want it to get around that you can bet thousands of dollars with him, using different names, then pay up whenever you feel like it."

"I know," Joey said. "You think I asked to get fired?"

"You owed this money before you got fired. What were you going to do, make two thousand dollars on this paycheck? Your bets have been out of control— betting those wild props and teases—or how about last year, betting on the fucking U.S. Open. I must be the biggest sucker in New York, taking tennis action from Joey DePino."

"I'll figure out a way to get you the money. I swear on my mother's grave."

"How?"

"I don't know."

"Well, you better think of something. You know how much I'm losing not being open tonight? Frank says I can't open up till he sees your money. I have rent to pay too you know."

"Tell me something, Morty," Joey said. He had been thinking about asking this question ever since Morty said Frank shut him down. "You lay off bets sometimes, don't you?"

"Not, personally," Morty said suspiciously, "Frank has a guy in the office usually takes care of that."

"Why I ask," Joey said, still not sure how to say it, "is I love, I mean I fucking love Indiana tonight. If there was a chapel I'd go fucking marry them. If they win—I mean *when* they win—I can pick up the money tomorrow morning and bring it right to you."

Morty stood up, looking angry and serious.

"What?" Joey said. "You don't believe me? Does this face look like it's lying?"

"Tomorrow," Morty said. "By noon. I don't care how you come up with that money, I don't care if you have to rob a goddamn bank, but you better come up with it somehow. I have enough *tsuras* in my life right now."

Morty put a five-dollar bill on the table and started to leave. Joey wanted to ask what *tsuras* meant, but instead he said, "Hey, Morty...Morty..."

Halfway toward the door, Morty turned around.

"You didn't even eat your Jello."

Joey watched Morty leave the diner.

Six

As soon as David left for work, Leslie called her mother in North Miami Beach.

"Don't worry," Elaine Schlossberg said, "all men go through a mid-life crisis sooner or later. I remember when your father read somewhere that dirt prevents cancer—he started eating a plateful of mud every morning for breakfast. I thought they'd have to take him away in a fishing net."

Leslie and her mother were very close. They spoke at least once a day and they knew everything about each other's lives. Recently, Leslie had been calling her mother even more often, worrying about David. He was constantly preoccupied, having trouble sleeping, obsessing about his health, and acting generally grumpy. Although he claimed it was just "things getting crazy at the office," Leslie knew it was something much more serious.

"It's just a phase," her mother assured her. "Your father doesn't eat dirt anymore, does he?"

But Leslie couldn't stop blaming herself.

Sometimes Leslie felt as if she and David were strangers, that he had no idea what she was really like.

Maybe this was because she did such a good job of hiding her real appearance. Mornings, while David was still asleep, Leslie would sneak into the bathroom, wash her face, and put on foundation, powder, and blush. She had been highlighting her hair various shades of blonde since she was fifteen and she went for a root perm every six months. Because she was convinced that her thighs were fat and unattractive, she always wore long blouses and sweaters. She didn't wear bikinis and she avoided the beach. She showered alone and, except occasionally when they were making love, she never let David see her naked. She'd already had a liposuction consultation for removing bulges on her stomach, hips and thighs, and she was planning to have the procedure done next year. Her teeth were capped and she'd had several light chemical skin peels. In high school, she'd had her first nosejob and several years ago she went for a second operation to have her nostrils narrowed. Now her nose was her favorite part of her body.

Throughout her life, people had always told Leslie that she was beautiful, but she never believed it. She knew that if it weren't for plastic surgery and high-maintenance she would be the below-average looking, chubby, rapidly aging woman with mousey brown hair, bad skin, and a big nose whom she imagined seeing in the mirror every day. But over the years Leslie had mastered the art of exuding confidence in public. When she was out with David or with her friends, she was always much more secure about herself than when she was alone. Only her mother had any idea how neurotic she was.

*   *   *

At around five o'clock, David called to say that he would be working late at the office and wouldn't be home until about eleven. This had been happening a lot lately. David had always been very involved in his career, but for the past month or two he seemed to prefer working than being home. Leslie feared this was because David wasn't attracted to her anymore. The past few years he'd been making more and more negative comments about her body. Once he told her that her thighs looked "blubbery." Another time he told her that she should "really think about joining a gym." Sometimes, when they were making love, David would squeeze the fat on Leslie's back or around her waist, making her self-conscious. He'd say he was doing it because he thought her fat was "sexy," but Leslie knew she repulsed him.

After Jessica went to sleep, Leslie went into the kitchen. Suddenly, she was starving. She opened a packet of Oreos and stuffed three cookies into her mouth at once. Realizing what she was doing and feeling guilty, she rushed into the bathroom. Just as she opened the lid of the toilet bowl and started to kneel down, she stopped herself. It was only a few cookies for God's sake—she had to stay in control, if not for her than for her family. Besides, skipping breakfast tomorrow would probably make up for it.

It was almost midnight and David still wasn't home from work, Leslie thought about calling him at his office, but he didn't like it when she disturbed him while he was working. Lately, anything she did seemed to disturb him.

Leslie decided to wait for David in bed. Watching an old movie put her to sleep quickly and she didn't wake up until David's weight shifted the mattress.

"What time is it?" Leslie asked.

"Never mind," David said. "Go back to bed."

David lay down next to Leslie, hugging her from behind. This happened all the time lately too—David would get into bed while Leslie was sleeping and hold her tight, but he never wanted to make love. Leslie turned around to face David and started kissing him. He kissed her back but without opening his mouth. She kissed his chin and under his neck. When she started to take off his T-shirt she realized that David had fallen asleep. She turned on to her back and started to cry.

*　*　*

In the morning, after David left for work, Leslie went into the kitchen and stuffed her mouth with whatever food her hands could grab. She started with the Oreos— sticking them into her mouth two or three at a time. Then she went for the leftover Halloween candy, unwrapping the miniature Snickers and Hershey bars with her nails and teeth, swallowing the bars half-chewed. Then she ate an entire jar of raspberry jelly, scooping up the globs with her fingers and sucking them clean. Only after she picked up a stick of butter did she realize exactly what she was doing. She dashed into the bathroom, glancing at her crazed expression in the mirror. She stood over the toilet and stuck a finger down her throat. She wretched and spit, but she couldn't get any food to come up. She imagined the five thousand calories of sugar and fat about to be absorbed into her body. Frantically, she grabbed a toothbrush and stuck the back end of it as far down her throat as it would go. Still nothing came up except a few globs of brown mucous. Staring at the mucous floating in the bowl, she was overcome by a sudden wave of nausea.

Afterwards, she imagined being hospitalized—tubes connected to her body, her face turning pale and ugly.

"Mom, I'm gonna be late for school."

"One second!" Leslie shouted.

She had almost forgotten that Jessica was still in the apartment. She wondered if she had heard her vomiting, afraid what type of psychological effect this could have on a child. Now she felt like she was a horrible wife *and* a horrible mother.

After brushing her teeth a few times, Leslie helped Jessica get ready for school. Quickly, she made a turkey sandwich and wrapped it in Saran Wrap. Jessica said, "Are you all right, mom?"

Jessica went to The Birch Wathen Lenox School where she excelled at everything and was involved in all of the ballet and theater performances. Jessica had straight brown hair and big brown eyes. Her nose was starting to grow but Leslie had already promised her a trip to a plastic surgeon for her sixteenth birthday.

"I'm fine," Leslie said. "I just didn't sleep very well last night."

"Is that why you were throwing up?"

Leslie didn't know what to say. She wanted to be honest with Jessica about everything, but she wasn't sure how to tell a ten-year-old girl about eating disorders.

"I think I just have a little virus," she said. "I'll be fine, sweetheart."

As they walked to school, Leslie felt terrible about lying. Jessica was extremely bright and she probably knew exactly what her mommy was doing in the bathroom. Maybe lying about it only gave Jessica the message that it's okay to make yourself throw up, as long as you do it in private.

After Leslie dropped off Jessica, she went to the

nearest kiosk on Second Avenue and bought a pack of cigarettes. She had never smoked before, except for a puff or two in college, and had always thought it was a disgusting, stupid habit. But lately she had been craving nicotine. It took her several tries to realize that you have to inhale on the end of a cigarette in order to light it. The first drags caused her to cough, but she finally got the hang of it. When the cigarette burnt down, she lit another.

As usual, men on the street harassed Leslie as she passed by. Some men whistled, others called her "beautiful" and "sexy." Leslie tried to block out all the noise and concentrate on her own thoughts. At times like this she always wondered what she was doing, living in New York. What was the point in having a lot of money and living in a great apartment if you couldn't even take a walk in your own neighborhood in peace? She was passing a homeless man rummaging through a big pile of garbage. Afraid the man would cough or spit on her, she sped up, holding her breath in disgust.

Leslie wished she had someplace to go today. Two afternoons a week, she volunteered at the Spence Chapin Thrift Shop on Third Avenue. She also worked at blood drives for the Red Cross and volunteered occasionally for The Jewish Guild for the Blind. After college, she worked for a public relations firm, but she quit her job after she got married. As far as she was concerned the women's movement was all about choices, and her choice was to stay at home. Besides, David was making plenty of money and she didn't see why she had to work if she didn't want to.

Although she had studied art history in college, Leslie always thought she would have made a great psychologist. Her own life might have been a mess, but she'd always been great at solving other people's problems. Even strangers seemed to benefit from her advice. Like yesterday afternoon at Macy's when that nice Chinese woman had complained about how she was in love with a man and didn't know how to make him love her back. As usual, Leslie had solid advice, telling the woman, "You have to be more aggressive with him. A lot of women are shy about what they want and I think that backfires. You finally have to put your foot down and say to yourself, 'This is what I deserve,' and then go out and get it."

Leslie walked up and down the side streets of the Upper East Side, window shopping in antique stores. She decided that her entire life was meaningless and that if she disappeared forever at this moment no one, except maybe Jessica, would miss her. By the time she decided it was too cold to be outside walking around, she had smoked half a pack of Marlboro Lights.

When she arrived back at her building, the day doorman, Robert, told her that she had received a delivery. From behind the desk, Robert retrieved a small padded envelope. There was no address on it, only the name LESLIE SUSSMAN, written with a black magic marker in block letters.

"Who delivered this?" she asked.

"Some guy," Robert said.

"A delivery man?"

"A black guy. I didn't get a good look at him. He said you were expecting it."

Leslie squeezed the envelope, but it had air-bubble padding and she couldn't feel whatever was inside.

In her apartment, Leslie put the envelope on the table and contemplated whether to open it. She had no idea what it could be. She wondered if she should wait for David to come home, or if she should just throw it down the trash chute. There were always stories in the news about the latest mail-bomber and she thought that maybe she should put the package in a pot of water.

Staring at the harmless-looking envelope, she decided that she was being crazy. It was probably just junk mail or a cosmetics company sending her a makeup sample. She tore open the envelope and discovered a mini-cassette. Now she was really confused. She checked again to see if there was any note with the package or a return address. She hesitated for a while, thinking, then decided she had nothing to lose. She found David's mini-cassette player on the bookshelf, put the cassette inside, and pressed PLAY.

Seven

JOEY DIDN'T HAVE to turn on the TV to know that Indiana had beaten Orlando. He knew they would win as soon as the game started and he hadn't gotten a bet in. Sure enough, in the morning, after Maureen had gone to work, he turned on ESPN's "Sports Center" and saw that Indiana had won by twenty-nine points. The game was never close. At half time, Indiana was up by twenty, and the closest Orlando ever came was in the fourth quarter when they cut the lead to sixteen.

Joey was furious at Morty. If Morty had given him the name of another bookie, Joey would have hit that bet, maybe hooked it up with a couple of other winners, and he'd have at least the two thousand bucks he needed to pay off Frank.

Joey sat in his underwear all morning watching television. He wasn't in the mood to start looking for a job and he had no place to go. Besides, it was Friday and jobs wouldn't be listed until the Sunday paper came out. He was probably at the lowest point in his life, but the thing that depressed him most was that he wouldn't be able to gamble again. He had no idea what he'd do today, tonight, and all future days and nights without having any action. He figured he'd be better off if someone just put a gun in his mouth and shot him.

At noon, Morty called. Joey told him that he didn't have the money and Morty started talking in Yiddish again.

"So what do you expect me to do?" Morty finally said. "Frank wasn't bullshitting. He wants his money today and he means it."

"If you let me put in that Indiana bet we wouldn't have a problem," Joey said.

"You and your cockamamie Indiana," Morty said. "What if they lost? Then you'd be in the hole to another bookie and Frank still wouldn't have his money."

"What can I tell you?" Joey said. "Tell Frank to call me and we'll make out a payment plan."

"Oh no you don't," Morty said. "Frank won't let me open up again until your debt is paid off—in full. You think I'm gonna sit around forever, waiting for you to come up with that money? I'll lay the money out, out of my own pocket. You'll pay it back as soon as you can, and I know you'll pay it back soon because I'm not putting in any more action until I get back every cent. And I'm gonna spread word around, to every other bookie I know, not to take your action."

Joey knew all along that Morty would lay out the money for him. It had nothing to do with Frank not letting him open up either. Joey knew that was just bullshit to try to scare him into coming up with the money. There was no way Frank would have ever said he wanted to "set an example" with him. It didn't matter how many girlfriends had dumped him, life wasn't like the movies. Bookies don't go pushing their clients around, especially for a few thousand bucks. Joey knew for a fact that Frank had a few players who bet fifty thousand dollars a night, and Frank wasn't going to waste his time strong-arming a small-potatoes player like himself.

But despite Morty bailing him out, Joey's money problems seemed never-ending. He still owed two other bookies, and then of course there was the debt to Carlos, the loan shark he'd borrowed a thousand bucks from about a month ago to make a payment to Morty. To Joey, this was the most significant debt of all because he owed an additional thirty percent for every week he didn't pay. The original debt had already increased to twenty-seven hundred dollars and, unlike bookies, loan sharks were serious about collecting unpaid debts. Their clients were usually degenerate gamblers like Joey, and loan sharks knew that the higher the debts went, the more unlikely they were to get paid.

There was also a stack of bills on the kitchen table. Maureen could take care of those but Joey usually paid half the rent and he had no idea where that money would come from.

It was all too depressing to think about. Without even a few dollars to go down to the deli and buy a sandwich for lunch, Joey had to scavenge in the kitchen, finally having a lunch of stale crackers and hardened cream cheese. Joey didn't know how some people sat home all day and watched television. ESPN had on woman's beach volleyball and Sports Channel was showing figure skating. Channel 71 showed live races from Aqueduct, but Joey wouldn't even flip to that station, knowing that watching horse racing without being able to bet would make him even more depressed.

Joey was watching an aerobics workout program—two blondes with nice racks jumping around in bikinis—when Maureen called from work.

"I just got a call from Leslie," she said. "She invited us over for dinner tonight."

"The *Sussmans*?" Joey said, like it was the name of a disease.

"I can tell her we can't make it," Maureen said, "but it's not like we have anything better to do."

"Fuck," Joey said, thinking about how boring it always was at the Sussmans'. Maureen and Leslie always started talking about their usual whatever, and he'd be stuck talking to Leslie's dorky husband. Besides, Joey didn't feel like being around other people tonight, especially after the week he'd had. He was about to tell Maureen to cancel when he remembered how broke and hungry he was and how dinner at the Sussmans' would at least mean a free meal.

"All right," he said. "If you want to go, I'll go."

Maureen came home from work at about five-thirty and, after she had changed and washed up, she and Joey left the apartment. They took the 1 train downtown to Times Square, then switched for the Shuttle and took the 6 train to Seventy-seventh Street. They hardly talked the whole way. On the Shuttle, Maureen told Joey a story about how one of the lawyers at work was leaving the firm, but Joey, thinking about his own problems, was hardly paying attention. Eventually, Maureen shut up.

As they walked up Seventy-ninth Street, past all the fancy, doorman buildings, Maureen suggested that they stop at a liquor store and buy a bottle of wine.

"We don't have to bring wine," Joey said.

"We can't show up empty-handed," Maureen said.

"You want wine, go buy wine," Joey said.

They went to a liquor store on Second Avenue and, while Joey waited outside, Maureen bought a bottle of red wine.

When Maureen came out she said, "I don't understand what's wrong with you."

Joey didn't answer. The truth was he didn't care one way or another about buying the wine, but he had been barely able to scrounge up money for subway tokens.

They went around the corner to David and Leslie's building. It was the fanciest building on the block and whenever they went over there Joey could always tell that Maureen was jealous. She didn't hide it very well, looking around the wood-panelled lobby like it was a room in a museum. After Maureen gave their names to the doorman who announced them, she and Joey didn't say another word until they were on the nineteenth floor, outside the Sussmans' door, and Maureen whispered, "Be nice, Joey."

*   *   *

David wasn't thrilled to hear that the DePinos were coming over for dinner, but he was glad he wasn't going to have to spend the night alone with Leslie. Only a few hours earlier he had thought he was going to die of a heart attack. It was moments after Leslie called him at his office and said that a mini-cassette had been delivered to the apartment building. He had felt a sudden pain in his chest and thought his left arm went numb. Out of breath, he managed to say, "Did you play it?"

"Yes, and that's the strangest part," Leslie said. "I played both sides and there was nothing on it at all. Who in the world would have sent me a blank cassette tape?"

Wondering what he had to do to make Amy leave him alone, David said, "I have no idea."

When he got home from work, Leslie showed him

the tape and the envelope with her name written in block letters. He tried to act as baffled over the mystery as she was, but he feared that he had given himself away. He had always been a terrible liar. Leslie often pointed out that she could always tell when he wasn't telling the truth because he didn't move his upper lip. Consciously trying to keep his upper lip mobile, David said, "Maybe some tape manufacturing company in the neighborhood is doing a promotion."

"A tape manufacturing company?" Leslie asked.

"You never know," David said. "They could be doing a promotion—got your name off of some list."

Leslie stared at David—he thought she was trying to read into him—and then said, "But why wouldn't they print envelopes for a promotion?"

David suggested a couple of other way-out possibilities, then said, "Who knows? Maybe you'll get more free gifts delivered," like the whole thing was a big joke.

When the doorbell rang, Leslie yelled from the kitchen for David to answer it. As soon as David saw Joey and Maureen, he knew something was wrong between them. Leslie was always telling him about the DePinos' marital problems and he guessed that they were probably in the middle of a fight. After they said their hellos, David led his guests through the short hallway into the living room where Jessica and a friend from the building were playing a Nintendo game on the TV.

"Why don't you two go into your room and do that, pumpkin," David said.

The children protested a few times, then marched out of the living room. Leslie called for Maureen to come into the kitchen and suddenly David and Joey were alone. David had always felt awkward around

Joey, the same way he felt awkward around all people who were uneducated or who made less money than he did. He always felt under pressure, as if the onus to come up with topics for conversation was on him.

"So I heard about your job," David said. "That really sucks."

"Word gets 'round fast," Joey said, eating some cashews he'd taken out of the bowl on the glass coffee table.

"I have several clients in the fiber-optic industry. I can put some feelers out for you if you want."

"It's all right," Joey said. "I don't think I'll have trouble finding something."

David watched Joey continue to eat cashews, four or five at a time. He was out of things to say and he was starting to wish that he'd put up a bigger stink about the DePinos coming over tonight.

Several seconds passed then Leslie and Maureen entered from the kitchen.

"Did you see?" Leslie said. "Joey and Maureen brought us a very nice bottle of red wine. Wasn't that nice of them?"

"Very nice," David said.

"But I think we should save it for another time," Leslie said. "Since we're having Chinese tonight I think we should really have a nice Japanese beer. Why don't you go around the corner to the deli and buy a couple of six packs?"

"You're kidding," David said.

"No, I'm serious. Why don't you see if they have some Sapporo? That would go very nicely."

"But it has to be twenty degrees out there."

"I really want it," Leslie said. "Why don't you take Joey with you?"

Now David realized what Leslie was getting at. Whenever she and Maureen got together they always liked to have private talks, like they were teenagers. David didn't feel like going anywhere, but he figured some fresh air might do him some good.

"Go with him, Joey," Maureen said. "Keep him company."

Joey's mouth was stuffed with cashews. He swallowed then said, "I'm happy right here."

David saw Maureen glare at Joey.

"You want to take a walk with me?" David said to Joey.

"Go with him, Joey," Leslie said.

"Whatever," Joey said, and he put a handful of cashews back into the bowl.

Joey and David stood in the hallway, waiting for the elevator, not saying anything to each other. Again David sensed the awkwardness, but he could tell Joey didn't think anything was wrong. David wondered what it would be like to be Joey, to be so oblivious to his feelings. It would be great to go through life that way, David figured—not to be affected by anything that happened around you, to always be cool and relaxed. David wondered what Joey would do if a woman like Amy Lee started threatening him and his family, and it occurred to David that Joey might be the perfect person to ask for some advice.

In the elevator David said to Joey, "You can't believe what's been going on with me lately," but, because there were a few other people in the elevator with them, he didn't tell Joey anything else until they were walking along Seventy-ninth Street. David felt like he had to be macho to talk to Joey, so he used language he wouldn't ordinarily use, saying things like "I fucked her on my desk" and "she really knows how to suck a dick, I'll tell you that much." Then he told Joey how Amy had become obsessive, threatening him lately, and how she'd sent the blank cassette to Leslie.

Joey didn't say a word until David stopped talking and then he said, "Why would you do a thing like that to Leslie?"

It wasn't the response David had been expecting. He'd expected Eric to get moralistic, but not Joey DePino.

"It wasn't supposed to be any big deal," David said, still trying to kiss-up to Joey. "I thought we'd just screw a few times and that would be the end of it."

"But weren't you thinking at all about your wife and little girl?"

"Not while I was doing it, no," David said defensively. He'd wished he'd kept his stupid mouth shut. For all he knew, Joey would go back to the apartment and tell Leslie. Even though the temperature was well below freezing and there was a stinging wind, David felt sweat building on his back.

"I don't understand how you could do a thing like that," Joey said.

"Well, I did," David said. "Maybe if you saw her you'd understand."

Joey still didn't seem impressed. He said, "Where the hell is this deli anyway? I'm freezing my fuckin' *tuchas* off out here."

David did a double-take, surprised to hear Joey using a Yiddish word.

"It's right up the block," David said.

They continued down First Avenue, past the Cowboy Bar, and went into the deli on the corner of Seventy-eighth Street. Joey waited by the register while David paid for the beer. David knew he should probably shut up, not tell Joey anything else, but now he felt like he needed Joey's validation. When they left the deli he said, "I was hoping you could give me some advice."

"Advice?" Joey said. "What kind of advice?"

"Advice on how to get out of my situation."

"My advice is not to run around on your wife anymore, that's what my advice is."

It occurred to David that Joey might just be jealous. After all, if he were trapped in a bad marriage like Joey was, he wouldn't want to hear about another guy getting lucky either.

"Of course I don't want to cheat on Leslie anymore," David said. "I feel just awful about the whole thing. The problem is Amy. I don't know how to keep her away from me."

"That's easy," Joey said, "stop leading her on."

"I'm not."

"You said you were the one who kept going back to her."

"That's when it first started. I mean last night she swore it would be the last time we ever fooled around, and then she sent that tape today."

"You mean you screwed her again—after she said all this shit?"

"It's not what you think," David said, angry that he still had to defend himself. "I mean I didn't have a choice. She sent me an E-mail at my office yesterday afternoon saying if I didn't come over she'd send Leslie the tape—the real tape. So I went over to her apartment, figuring maybe I could reason with her. She lives in this tiny one-bedroom way down in the West Village, on Morton Street. When I get there, she's dressed like a hooker. I mean she has on fishnet stockings, red pumps, lipstick—you name it. I tell her it's over, but she keeps coming on to me. Finally, something I say reaches her and she stops looking crazy. She seems like a normal, reasonable person, and she tells me how she's been under an incredible amount of stress lately, and she never meant to do anything to hurt me. She said something like 'It was only because I loved you so much, but now I realize it's over.' So I think, 'Great, I'm starting to make some progress.' Then she says 'Make love to me one last time and I swear I'll never bother you again.' Of course I say no, but then she starts getting angry again so I figure—maybe this is the only way to get rid of her. So I say that I'll do it, but only if she promises that it'll definitely be the last time. Then, next thing I know, she's sending a cassette to Leslie."

David wasn't sure whether Joey was paying attention to him anymore. They had turned back on to Seventy-ninth Street, heading toward David's building.

"Let's just get the hell back to the apartment," Joey said, walking with his head down against the wind, his hands deep inside his jacket pockets.

* * *

Leslie and Maureen were in the kitchen, transferring the Chinese food that Leslie had ordered for dinner out of the cartons onto serving plates. Leslie and David had recently put in brand-new pine cabinets in the kitchen. The bathroom had also been remodeled with new marble tile and in the living room they had gotten a huge armoire from Domain in the Trump Palace. Maureen hated Leslie for having all the things she'd ever wanted.

"I think you're making a mistake," Leslie said, scooping out the steamed vegetables and other oil-free dishes she had ordered. "Losing his job has nothing to do with you. You have to think about what is right for Maureen Byrne."

Leslie always called Maureen by her maiden name when she wanted to make a point about how much she hated Joey.

"I know you're right," Maureen said. "I guess I'm hoping a miracle happens and all my problems just go away. What I'd give for one week, just one week, with Joey home every night, when I didn't have to worry about where he was."

Leslie's hand froze, holding a ladle full of steamed chicken and broccoli.

"You mean you didn't give him the ultimatum?"

"I tried to but then he told me he lost his job and I just couldn't."

Leslie continued to dish out the food.

"You know I can't understand you," Leslie said. "How could you let a guy push you around like that?"

"I can't help it."

Leslie shook her head.

"You know what you have to do, just do it."

"I don't know if I can."

"He won't change."

"I know that. I still can't."

"You like suffering?"

"No."

"You want kids? You want a nice place to live?"

"Yes."

"Then you only have one choice."

"I know what you're saying. I mean I'm hearing you."

"I'm going to say something now and I'm probably wrong, and you'll probably just think I'm crazy, but I'm going to say it anyway. Did you ever wonder if maybe Joey wasn't gambling as much as you thought he was?"

"What do you mean?"

"Think about it a second. You say he's out late all the time, doesn't say where he's going. Maybe he's..."

"Joey?"

"I'm just suggesting—"

"You're crazy."

"Think about it. It's not impossible."

"What woman would be interested in Joey?"

"You're interested in him."

Five years ago, Maureen thought. Not since he started going to the track every night, acting like a jerk all the time.

Leslie carried a platter of food through the swinging door into the dining room. Maureen followed her, carrying a large serving bowl of brown rice. She said, "I still think you're crazy."

Leslie said, "Remember in high school, when you were so screwed up because you had all those problems with your father? I used to have to beat it into you, again and again, until you finally realized what he was doing to you. It's the same way with Joey. He's the crazy one, he has the problems, not you. Maybe I can see things that you can't or don't want to see."

Maureen tried to picture Joey and another woman. She saw his hairy body glistening with sweat in some cheap hotel room. Somehow she couldn't get the picture to seem real.

"I appreciate how you're trying to help me, but I really don't think it's the problem."

"Even so," Leslie said, "maybe you should start to, you know—keep your eyes open."

Following Leslie back through the swinging door, Maureen said, "What do you mean?"

"Tomorrow, when you're walking on the street,

smile at the first good-looking guy you pass. See what happens."

"Nothing'll happen."

"How do you know?"

"I look in the mirror. I know what I look like."

"Don't be ridiculous—you're beautiful."

"I'm fat."

Now Leslie stared at Maureen seriously, holding her gaze for a few seconds, and then she said, "Just try it. It could open your eyes—make you see what a pig you're married to."

Leslie exited the kitchen. Maureen remained, imagining herself with a handsome, considerate man, a good provider and a good husband—someone like David. Maureen had always thought that David would make the perfect husband—he was kind, attractive, intelligent and, most importantly, dependable. She imagined living with David in a three-bedroom, two-bath apartment, with big windows overlooking Central Park, snuggling in bed all day, or just sitting on the couch together watching TV, spending lazy nights at home like married people were supposed to. And they'd have children too—a pretty little girl like Jessica and a boy named Shaun. Maureen had always wanted to name a boy Shaun after Shaun Cassidy, her teenage idol, who she still thought was the most gorgeous man who had ever lived.

"Are you all right?"

Maureen hadn't even noticed that Leslie had come back into the kitchen.

"Fine," Maureen said, wondering what it would feel like to kiss Shaun Cassidy, or anyone who wasn't Joey.

* * *

As David gave his lame excuse for why he was cheating on his wife, Joey was thinking about his bowling ball. It was a Brunswick ball and had to be worth at least fifty bucks, maybe seventy-five. Plus he had his golf clubs and some old baseball cards in his closet. He had a sixty-six Mickey Mantle he once got from some kid's older brother in fourth grade, plus hundreds of other cards from the early seventies. If he could scrape up a couple hundred bucks he could go to the Meadowlands tomorrow night and turn it into a few thousand. He sure as hell wasn't going to make any money sitting on his couch another day.

When David finished talking Joey said, "Let's just get the hell back to the apartment."

Joey didn't know why David was telling him all about his stupid affair anyway. They had never been very friendly, hardly even talking all the times the two couples had gotten together. Once, David was looking to buy a TV set and Joey told him to buy a Zenith instead of an R.C.A., so they talked a little bit. Another time they had a conversation about the Yankees. David said he was a big Yankee fan, but then it turned out he thought Sparky Lyle and Reggie Jackson were still on the team. David was just a big-time dork, no two ways about it. But the thing that really ticked Joey off was the way David was always so phony, trying to act like he was someone he wasn't. Who was he kidding talking about how he "fucked her on the desk" and "she really knows how to suck a dick," like he wasn't some uppity advertising schmuck.

Joey really couldn't give a shit about David and his stupid problem. Obviously, the guy was just looking for trouble, starting up with this Chinese broad in the first place. Guys like David, they had so much money, they had to invent things to worry about. Why else would a guy with a little blonde wife like Leslie, who still had a nice high rack after pumping out a kid, go out looking for some action on the side? Even nuttier—what would some good-looking Chinese girl want with David? Joey was willing to bet good money that she didn't look as good as David said. She was probably some hag, like the ones who work behind the counter at the Korean delis.

In the elevator, David said, "You won't tell Leslie or Maureen about any of this, will you? What I mean is, I can trust you, right?"

Joey gave David his famous "Don't-you-think-I-have-anything-better-to-do-with-my-life?" stare. The fucking dork had no idea what it was like to have real problems.

When they got back into the apartment, Joey had a feeling that Maureen and Leslie had been talking about him. Knowing how Leslie had always hated his guts, Joey doubted they had a lot of good things to say. Maureen probably complained about how he was still gambling all the time, and Leslie probably told her how she should get a divorce. Although Joey often wondered what it would be like to get Leslie in the sack—along with her nice rack she had big blow-job lips and she had that kind of slutty wave in her blonde hair—he hated her personality. What kind of woman invites a couple over for dinner and then orders in steamed Chinese food? And Joey didn't like the way she talked to Maureen, like she thought she was so much better than her. Maureen always said Joey was crazy, that Leslie was her best and closest friend, but Joey knew that Leslie was the type of friend that seems like she's there for you, but then disappears when you really need her.

During dinner, Joey tried not to pay much attention

to the conversation. He was concentrating instead on his food, trying to forget that it tasted like horse shit. Just because David was such a health food freak, everybody had to eat vegetables like a bunch of rabbits. David and Maureen didn't talk much either. It was mainly Leslie going on and on about how much more she had to do to get the apartment the way she wanted it, and how she was looking forward to going to Florida in April to visit her parents, and how "wonderfully" Jessica was doing in school. Joey looked at Leslie a couple of times, not because he was interested in what she was saying, but because a button on her blouse had popped open and the tops of her freckled tits were showing.

The worst part of the night was after dinner when Jessica and her friend performed their "show." Whenever Joey and Maureen came over, Jessica, and sometimes a friend, tortured them with some stupid act that they made up. They would dress up in Leslie's clothes and say stupid things and everyone would tell them how wonderful they were. Tonight they came out wrapped in towels and pretended to do a shampoo commercial. Joey thought it was as pathetic as usual, but everyone else clapped at the end, encouraging the poor kids. Joey wanted to tell them that they sucked Easter eggs, just to see everyone's faces.

When Jessica came and sat on Leslie's lap and Leslie kissed the top of her head, Joey saw Maureen looking at him. Right away he recognized her "Why-don't-we-have-any-children?" stare, and Joey glared back with his classic "I-don't-want-to-fuckin'-talk-about- it." Joey was getting sick of this—Maureen acting like he was so against having kids. The truth was he wanted to have kids some day as badly as she did. He wanted to take Joey Junior to Yankee Stadium and manage his little league games. But he knew how he would've hated growing up in some shit-hole apartment near Hell's Kitchen. A kid needs a house, a backyard, places to hang out. After he paid off all his gambling debts, Joey figured he could start putting some money away, maybe save up for a down payment on a house in Staten Island or Jersey. He'd explained all this to Maureen many times—not about the gambling debt, but about saving up money—and Maureen always said that he was just using this as an excuse, that he was just putting off having kids until she was too old or couldn't have any. So Joey decided not to even talk about it anymore. When the time was right, he'd bring it up himself, but until then he didn't care how many puppy-dog faces she made.

Finally, after coffee and fruit salad, it was time to go home. Leslie and Maureen had their usual phoney conversation at the door, telling each other what great times they both had, and how they had to do this again soon. Then Joey shook David's hand—of course he had a weak, wimpy handshake—and, as always, when he went to kiss Leslie, she backed away like he had the plague.

Riding down in the elevator, Maureen wasn't talking to him. Joey assumed it had to do with having kids which was fine by him. On the street, Maureen said, "Let's take a cab home."

"Can't afford it," Joey said.

"You don't expect me to take a subway at eleven at night?"

"What's wrong with the bus?"

Then Maureen marched into the street, waving her hand above her head, and a cab screeched toward the sidewalk.

"You're paying for this, right?" Joey said after he sat

down inside.

Maureen still wasn't talking to him and Joey knew she was still pissed about something. Women were unbelievable the way they always expected men to know exactly what they were thinking, like they thought men were fucking mind-readers or something.

Not until they were speeding along the curvy Seventy-ninth street crossway through Central Park did Maureen say, "Why do you have to be such a jerk all the time?"

Joey had no idea what she was talking about. All he knew was that it was past eleven on Friday night after a shitty week and he didn't feel like having another argument about kids. So he decided not to say anything —let Maureen brood until she forgot what she was upset about.

But Maureen wouldn't let it go.

"I think you don't appreciate me," she said. "I think that's what your problem is."

"Appreciate you?" Joey said. "What the hell are you talking about? Were you and Leslie talking about me before?"

"You'll see," Maureen said.

Joey wondered if Maureen was bleeding. That would explain why she was acting so nutso. But then he remembered that she'd been on the rag just last week, and he wondered if women could bleed twice in the same month. He never heard of it happening, but you never know.

As the cab swung around Columbus Circle, Joey decided that Maureen was probably upset about her father again. Whenever she started acting crazy she'd tell him that it really had to do with something her father did to her as a kid and he'd say, "Why didn't you tell me that in the first place?" and she'd say, "Because I thought you knew."

Women.

When they got back to their apartment the phone was ringing. Joey answered, wondering who could be calling so late.

"Joey?"

"Who's this?"

"Who's this?"

"I said who the fuck is this?"

"Never mind that. If this is Joey DePino you better just be outside—right now, man, or your lady's gonna get it."

Before Joey could say another word the Spanish-sounding guy had hung up.

"Who was that?" Maureen asked, still in a pissy mood.

"Prank caller," Joey said.

Maureen went into the bedroom and Joey stayed in the kitchen, wondering what to do. The voice hadn't sounded at all familiar, but he knew it had something to do with his debts. Frank wouldn't bother to send someone after him, but Carlos, his loan shark, might.

Joey hardly knew Carlos. A guy at the OTB on Thirty-seventh and Seventh introduced them, after he overheard Joey talking to another guy about how he needed to come up with a quick thousand bucks.

"You need money, you need Carlos," the guy had said.

He took Joey to the back of the OTB where there was a soup and candy counter. Standing next to the counter was a little old Puerto Rican guy with thick gray hair, eating a bowl of clam chowder. He only looked at Joey one time, then asked how much money he needed. Joey said one thousand dollars, and then Carlos explained his interest rate (thirty percent a week), his payment plan (at least fifty every Wednesday), and his conditions (miss one payment and the whole debt is due). Then he asked Joey for his address and phone number, which he must have memorized because he never stopped eating his chowder.

Carlos told Joey to meet him in the OTB bathroom in five minutes. Joey went in, then Carlos came in, handed him a wad of hundreds, checked his hair in the mirror, then walked out.

That was a little over a month ago. Joey had only missed one payment to Carlos—two days ago—and he'd been planning to go ask for an extension tomorrow or the day after.

Joey decided that he better go outside. Carlos had seemed like a reasonable guy. He probably just wanted to see Joey's face, make sure he hadn't skipped town or lied about his address and phone number.

Joey grabbed a plastic shopping bag full of trash and told Maureen he was taking out the garbage. From the vestibule, Joey couldn't see anybody outside, and he wondered whether it had been a prank call after all. But then when he stepped out in front of the building he noticed two young guys—one black, one Spanish-looking—standing in front of a dark blue Ford. Joey had never seen the Spanish guy before, but the black guy's face looked familiar. He had seen him around at the Thirty-seventh Street OTB, and also at the branch on Seventy-second Street. He was usually with a bunch of other black guys—West Indians—and Joey never knew he had anything to do with Carlos.

Joey stood in front of his building, wondering what to do. He noticed another guy in the Ford, behind the steering wheel. He looked around to see if there was a cop, or anyone else who might be able to help him, but there was only an old homeless guy standing with his cup outside the deli. The black guy was in a big blue down jacket and looked like the Michelin Man. He lifted up the bottom of the jacket, revealing the handle of a handgun that was tucked under his pants. The Spanish guy, in a black leather biker's jacket, didn't move.

"Get the fuck over here," the black guy said. He didn't sound West Indian.

Joey thought about trying to get back into the apartment building. It was only about five yards away, but even if he made it into the vestibule there was no way he was going to be able to find his key and open the inside door before one of the guys caught him. So Joey decided he might as well go over there, just to see what they wanted. After all, the gun was just for intimidation. Loan sharks might play hardball, but they weren't gonna shoot somebody for a couple thousand bucks.

Joey came over and stopped about five feet away. The black guy, still holding the gun inside his jacket, said, "Closer" and Joey walked a few steps farther. He was so close he could see that the Puerto Rican guy had missed a spot shaving on the bottom of his chin. The black guy smelled like tomato sauce. He decided that they were twenty-one years old, tops.

"You got twenty-seven hundred bucks?" the black guy said.

"So that's what this is all about," Joey said, deciding to play dumb. "I knew I seen you around the OTB, but I never knew you worked for Carlos."

"My man axed you a question," the Puerto Rican guy said, "so you might as well answer it." Joey noticed that the Puerto Rican guy had an under-bite, his bottom teeth sticking up like Dracula's fangs, and his breath smelled like tomato sauce too.

"Hey, there's no big deal with this here," Joey said. "I know you guys are just doing your job and everything, but you don't gotta worry—I'm good for Carlos' money. I was gonna stop by and talk to him tomorrow."

"You still didn't answer my man's question," the Puerto Rican guy said. "You got that money or don't you?"

"No," Joey said. "But I'll have it—no problem."

The black guy pushed Joey back and said, "Walk."

"Walk?" Joey said. "Walk where?"

"You heard my man," the Puerto Rican guy said. "Just walk."

Joey walked toward the corner with the two guys following behind him, and Joey wondered whether they were crack heads—if they killed guys just for looking at them the wrong way. They steered him around the corner to Fifty-fourth Street. It was a dark, quiet block with warehouses and parking lots.

"You gotta be kiddin' me," Joey said. "You sure you're not makin' a mistake, confusing me with some other guy. I'm Joey DePino. I owe Carlos a couple thousand bucks—that's it."

The guys didn't say anything, just kept nudging Joey along. When they were in the middle of the block, where the bulb was out in the lamppost, they stopped and pushed Joey against a brick wall. The black guy took his hand out of his pocket, but he wasn't holding the gun. He was holding a box-cutter up to Joey's face.

"You think I'm playin' with you, man?"

He ran the blade slowly up and down Joey's face, then he cut a small "X" into the breast of Joey's Giants jacket. A second later, Joey felt a sharp pain in his face, on his left cheekbone, and only then did he realize that the Puerto Rican guy was punching him. Joey keeled over, holding his face, and then felt a sharp, nauseating pain in his stomach, someone punching or kicking him. There was more pain, but Joey was trying to block it all out, thinking about flowers. That's what his mother always told him to do whenever he had nightmares. It didn't work when he was a kid and it didn't work now.

Joey couldn't believe that this was the way he was gonna check out—murdered, shot by a couple of crack heads in the middle of a dark street. He always thought he'd die in bed, an old man with Maureen and maybe his grand kids watching over him. Then he started wondering about what his last thought would be.

Finally, the attack stopped. Joey lay on the ground in a fetal position, trying to stay as still as possible. Afraid if he moved the guys would start kicking him again. He heard the Puerto Rican guy say, "Let's go, D."

The black guy said, "Wait up, I don't think we got him enough yet," and Joey felt another blow to his rib cage.

The Puerto Rican guy said, "D, 'fore somebody sees us."

The black guy said to Joey, "This is just a taste of what you gonna get if Carlos don't have all his money next Friday."

"D," the Puerto Rican guy said.

Suddenly, it was quiet. Joey didn't move. Lying there on the ground, tasting blood on his lips, he saw a perfect rose.

Eight

JOEY EXPLAINED TO Maureen how a homeless guy outside
the deli had jumped him for absolutely no reason. When
he was telling the story, he didn't think there was any
way in the world Maureen would buy it, but amazingly
she believed every word.

"You have to go to the hospital," she said
hysterically. "You have to get an AIDS test."

"Don't you read the papers?" Joey said. "Hospitals
are where people *catch* AIDS."

"You never know," Maureen pleaded, "he was
probably a drug addict—he could've scratched you with
a needle. Please don't be an idiot—let me take you to the
hospital."

"Forget about it," Joey said, "and I'm not calling the
cops neither. They don't care about homeless guys. If
they even look for him, they'll arrest him and then I'll
have to show up in court. I don't want to deal with that
shit."

Joey got up from the couch, still holding the ice
wrapped in a dish towel over his face. His ribs and legs
hurt like hell, but he didn't think anything was broken,
and the last thing he wanted was to get the police

involved. What would he say to the cops, "My loan shark's friends beat me up," and give a full description of the two guys? They might have pushed Joey around to get Carlos' money back, but Joey knew they'd probably kill him if he ratted to the cops. And the last thing he wanted was Maureen to find out about the money he'd borrowed. Gambling was one thing, but he knew if Maureen ever found out exactly how much money he owed and that he'd gotten mixed up with a loan shark, that would be the absolute last straw.

Joey had to lay on his back all night. He only slept for short spurts and spent most of the night half-awake and half-dreaming, re-experiencing each punch and kick, but imagining the attack had taken place at the Meadowlands, right after the INQUIRY sign had been posted. A few times during the night Maureen asked him if he was okay and each time he told her he was fine, to just go back to sleep and forget about him. Meanwhile, the pain in his face was so bad it hurt when he moved his lips to talk.

In the morning, Maureen looked at him as if she had woken up next to a monster.

"I can't believe I listened to you last night," she said, "we're going to a doctor right this second."

Joey told Maureen that she was crazy and he wasn't going anywhere—until he tried to get out of bed. His ribs hurt so much he could hardly move, and when he finally got up and looked at himself in the mirror he barely recognized his face. It was purple and red and some spots were still bleeding. Maureen said she would pay for a cab and she and Joey went downtown to the emergency room at St. Vincent's Hospital. It took a couple of hours before anyone would see him, and then the doctor on duty ordered x-rays. Later, he determined

that Joey's ribs were just bruised, but that he needed
stitches on two parts of his face. The doctor suggested
that Joey go see a plastic surgeon because the wounds
were in such visible spots—one below his right eye, the
other on the left side of his face, near his mouth. But
Joey said he was willing to take his chances and he let
an emergency room doctor sew the stitches.

Finally, at a little after one o'clock, Joey returned to
the waiting room where Maureen was still sitting,
reading magazines.

"Aren't you glad I brought you here now?" Maureen
said.

"I owe you one," Joey said. He hadn't told her that
he'd rejected the option to go to a plastic surgeon. "If it's
all right with you, I'll see you a little later."

"Where are you going?" Maureen said, implying
that she knew he was going gambling.

"Don't worry, I'm not doing nothing like that," Joey
said. "I just thought I'd hit the pavement, start looking
for a job."

"On Saturday?"

"I know a guy—remember Mike Diaz?—we worked
a few jobs together. I figure he might know something
or maybe there's something for me at the company he's
at out in Jersey."

"Why can't you call him?" Maureen asked.

"I will, but I want to see him in person, try to kiss-
up to him a little. Don't worry, I'll be home by five tops."

Outside the hospital, Maureen headed north, up
Seventh Avenue, while Joey headed crosstown on West
Eleventh Street. Of course Joey had no intention of
calling Mike Diaz. He hadn't even spoken to Mike in
nearly three years. He had no idea where Mike was
working and he would never even think of asking for

his help finding a job. He wasn't planning to go gambling either because while he was waiting for the doctor to come sew his stitches he'd decided that the chances of turning any money he made from the sale of his bowling bowl, golf clubs, and some old baseball cards into enough to pay off his debts were about one in a million. Joey knew he had to come up with another idea, and he wasn't gonna get any thinking done sitting home all day with Maureen.

Joey made a left on Broadway and headed toward Union Square Park. It wasn't as cold as it had been lately. Bright sunshine made it hard to look straight ahead without squinting and the wind had died down. The small park was emptier than it would have been in warmer weather, but a few people were out walking their dogs and the usual zombies were wandering around, searching through the garbage bins or mumbling to themselves. Joey was oblivious to everything except his own thoughts, and he didn't become aware of his surroundings again until he was sitting down at the end of a bench, on the only part that wasn't spotted with bird shit.

Joey was thinking about the idea that had been in the back of his mind since last night, when he was lying awake in bed. The biggest problem was he didn't know how he could rob Tech Systems and get away with it. He was pretty sure he could get into the building at night through the main entrance. He was also confident that once he reached the fourth floor he could pick the locks to the Tech Systems' office. A guy he knew in high school who used to break into all the teachers' offices and steal tests had once taught Joey how to pick locks with a safety pin. After a lot of practice, Joey had gotten pretty good at it. He'd never tried to pick the Tech Systems' locks, but he knew they were two standard

Arrow locks and he didn't see where there would be any trouble. The biggest problem would be getting in and out without being seen by one of the in-office security cameras. There were cameras in five places that Joey knew about. And even if he managed to get in and out of the office without being seen he wasn't sure exactly what he would take. Computer equipment was too bulky to steal and any cash was secured in a safe. The only things he could think of were a couple of IBM Think Pads and some computer memory. There were memory cards in the computers in the supply room in the back, but taking the cards would mean dismantling the computers, which could take hours. And once Joey had the memory cards he wasn't sure exactly what he would do with them. They could be worth thousands of dollars, but they weren't something he could unload easily on the street.

It frustrated Joey not being able to come up with a plan to rob Mark Conine blind because he would have loved to do something to hurt that rich stuck-up bastard. He imagined Mark showing up for work on Monday morning, seeing all his computers in pieces on the floor. The wimp wouldn't know what to do. He would probably go right to the phone and start crying to his mommy.

Joey took a deep breath, causing sharp pains in his ribs. X-rays had shown no breaks, but the way Joey felt he couldn't believe it. Rather than sitting straight up, which would have made him feel better, Joey crouched forward, trying to make the pain as bad as possible. He told himself that he deserved to be in pain for the way he had screwed up his life. If he kept feeling the pain maybe he'd remember what it was like the next time he wanted to go out and bet money he didn't have.

As the pain grew even more unbearable, Joey thought about David Sussman. Now there was a guy who'd never felt any pain. He had a skinny, big-titted wife, he was making a ton of money, and he lived in a fucking palace. Then he goes out and starts screwing some chick in his office and he thinks that's what suffering is. If he wanted to know suffering, let him go to the track one night and hit a seventeen-thousand-dollar number and then have the INQUIRY sign light up. Or let him get a call in the middle of the night from some guys who wanted to rearrange his face. Or let him get fired from his job and have no money in the bank and debts up the wazoo and then come home to a nagging wife with a bum ovary and a bone up her ass. Let him spend one day as Joey DePino and then he'd know what pain was all about.

Joey couldn't take it anymore. He sat up, trying to catch his breath. Then he imagined what Monday morning would be like, standing on the unemployment line. He had nothing against taking free money from the government, but a couple of hundred bucks a week wasn't gonna get him out of the hole he was in. He needed fast money, big money, he needed...

It was so simple he didn't know why he hadn't come up with the idea sooner. There was one person he could get money from, and a lot of it too. And he wouldn't have to borrow the money from him, or steal it. There was a much easier way and Joey didn't have any doubt that it would work. The only problem was he needed help, but maybe that wasn't a problem. His old friend Billy Balls owed him a favor anyway.

* * *

Amy Lee, wearing dark sunglasses and with her hair pulled back into a tight ponytail, followed Leslie into the Gristede's supermarket on Second Avenue and Seventy-fifth Street. Amy knew from watching Leslie the past two weeks that she went food shopping on Sundays before noon. Unlike the past two Sundays when it was freezing, it was comfortable standing in the sun on Seventy-ninth Street, waiting for Leslie to leave her building.

She followed Leslie into the frozen food section where she picked out five Weight Watchers frozen dinners. Then she watched her select a carton of skim milk and containers of fat-free yogurt and fat-free cottage cheese. In the dressing room at Macy's, Amy had seen Leslie in her underwear and she didn't see what was so special about her body. She had an okay figure, but she didn't look like she worked out a lot or went blading. Her arms were too thin and she had all sorts of dimples on her thighs. Amy knew that she was much better looking than Leslie, and she knew that David knew it too.

As Leslie was squeezing grapefruits, Amy was squeezing the grip of the .32 in her coat pocket. She'd bought the gun two years ago after a man followed her home one night from the ATM machine on Seventh Avenue and Christopher Street. After robbing her at knife-point, he tried to rape her in the vestibule of her apartment building. He had pulled up her skirt and sliced off her panties when two drunk college kids came by and scared the guy off.

Amy swore that she'd never be caught so defenseless again. The next morning, she went to the shooting range on Murray Street and started taking target practice. Her male instructor told her that he'd never seen a woman with a shooting hand so steady. Eventually, Amy could hit any target she aimed at. The day she got her permit she bought her gun at a store on Warren Street. The next time a guy cornered her she was going to blow him away, which was exactly what happened last Christmas Eve.

She was on her way home from this party someone at work was having when she noticed this skinny black guy following her. When she turned on to Morton Street the guy got closer, and as soon as she felt the guy's hand touch her shoulder she turned and fired twice—one shot into his face, the other into his chest as he was falling backwards. The next day the murder was reported everywhere, but there were no witnesses. It turned out the dead guy was a wanted serial rapist who had committed at least six brutal rapes in the West Village. Amy doubted that the police would try very hard to find the killer. Sure enough, the case went unsolved.

Amy blamed her problems with relationships on her parents' divorce. When she was four, her father had left—going back to China—and the shrink she'd gone to one time told her that she was trying to mimic her unstable childhood in her adult relationships. She always thought that psychotherapy was bullshit, but she had to admit that she had a knack for picking losers. When she was a teenager and in her early twenties she only dated Chinese guys to make her mother happy. But after a series of failed relationships she started dating white and Latino men too. The most serious boyfriend she'd ever had was a guy named Phil. He was a graduate student in bio-chemical engineering at NYU. They dated steadily for two years then, out of the blue, he announced that he was getting back together with his old girlfriend. Amy was so devastated she didn't date again for almost a year and when she started seeing guys again she felt damaged. She knew guys just wanted to use her and she didn't trust anybody.

When she was alone, she couldn't stop thinking about David. Just imagining him, home with his happy little family, was torture for her. Finally, she couldn't stand it anymore. She got David's home phone number from a guy in his department, and she started calling his apartment during the day, hanging up whenever his wife answered. She started to hate Leslie Sussman's voice. It was the cocky, self-assured voice of a woman who felt she was entitled to the best of everything. She'd hear the voice—*Hello? Hello?*—during the day at work, and in the middle of the many nights when she couldn't sleep.

She started following David. She'd leave the office ahead of him, then wait outside the office building until he got into a cab. Then she'd get into another cab and follow him home. When David got out, she'd watch him go into his building, and she wouldn't leave until the elevator doors closed.

Last Saturday night, she followed the entire Sussman family into an Italian restaurant on Second Avenue. She had put on a blonde wig and wore sunglasses so David didn't recognize her, even though she was eating only two tables away. On the surface, David seemed happy with his little family—laughing, holding hands with his wife, occasionally kissing his daughter on the head—but Amy knew how miserable he was inside.

When David told Amy he wanted to end the affair, Amy was naturally upset. She hoped that it was just cold feet, that he didn't mean what he was saying. What other explanation could there be? She didn't want to threaten him the way she did, but what choice did she have? So Amy took off work the next morning and followed his wife Leslie to the Manhattan Plaza. She photographed Leslie having lunch with a friend, then she followed her into Macy's and spoke to her in the dressing room. Amy didn't enjoy showing David that picture, but when David agreed to come to her apartment the next night, Amy knew her strategy had worked. David's anger was only a facade, hiding his true feelings, and Amy knew she could gradually reveal the real David Sussman.

After they had sex that night Amy was convinced that she was making progress, that there was no way David would give her up to return to his stuck-up wife. Then, getting dressed, David pulled the same crap that he'd pulled in his office, saying that the affair was over and that she had to start leaving him and his family alone. Now Amy wasn't sure whether it was just cold feet. It seemed as if David really meant what he was saying, and Amy couldn't understand this. Because if he meant what he was saying now, that meant he was lying before, when he'd made all those promises.

One night last week, David and Amy had just made love and they were lying next to each other on the floor in David's office. It was so romantic the way David had his face pressed against Amy's neck and Amy was running her fingers slowly through David's sweaty chest hair. Then Amy realized that David was crying. She asked him what was wrong, but for a long time he wouldn't say anything. She decided not to pressure him; he would tell her what was on his mind when he was ready. Amy felt very motherly, kissing David's forehead, assuring him that everything was going to be all right.

Finally, David started telling Amy about his awful panic attacks. He said that he'd been having them for years, but that lately they were getting worse. He said that he sometimes felt "a clicking" in his chest and then he felt like he couldn't breathe. Then his heart would race out of control and he'd feel like he was going to die. He'd gone to doctors for it, but nothing they suggested helped, and when he told his wife about it she'd always tell him that he was "just being a hypochondriac." David continued to cry and Amy hugged him, assuring him that everything was going to be all right. Then David opened up to her completely. He told her how he felt trapped in his marriage, that he felt like time was passing him by, and that he was sick of going through life feeling afraid. Amy told David that he didn't have to worry anymore, that she would help him get over his fear. And that was when he told her how wonderful she was and how no woman had ever understood him the way she did. Then he squeezed her hands and looked into her eyes and said, "Will you marry me someday?"

Just thinking about that moment made Amy's face get hot. She knew that those were David's true feelings, that everything he had said *since* that night were the lies. Now David was just panicking again, feeling trapped and afraid; Amy knew that only she could help him and she knew exactly how to go about it.

Following Leslie up the canned-food aisle, Amy squeezed the gun even tighter, her index finger shaking on the trigger. Her intention wasn't to hurt Leslie. She hoped that other techniques would work and that Leslie and David would eventually split up peacefully. The last thing Amy wanted was to do something stupid and wind up in jail and let Leslie have David. In that case, she would have to do something really stupid and kill

David too, because if he spent the rest of his life with some other woman, that would be just as awful as if he stayed married to Leslie.

Leslie was reaching for a can of tomato paste. Amy was behind her, wondering if she should forget about playing it safe. Maybe she should just shoot Little Miss Prissy in the back—get it over with.

* * *

Leslie didn't recognize the young Chinese woman who had just called out her name. Only when the woman took off her sunglasses and said, "Remember me—the Macy's dressing room?" did it all click.

"My God, how are you?" Leslie said. "Do you live around here?"

"No," Amy said.

"This is so funny. I didn't recognize you right away, you did something to your hair, right? So, tell me, how did it go with your boyfriend? Did you take my advice?"

"Yes, I did actually," Amy said. "I've been a lot more aggressive with him lately and I think it's really starting to pay off."

"That's so wonderful. I'm very happy for you." Leslie paused a moment, squinting. "By the way, how did you know my name?"

"What do you mean?"

"I don't remember. Did I tell you it the other day?"

"You may have," Amy said. "Or maybe I just guessed it."

Leslie was confused. She was starting to feel uncomfortable around this woman and she wasn't sure why.

"I guess I should explain," Amy continued. "You see, I'm a psychic."

"Really?" Leslie said. "I don't think I've ever met a psychic before."

Amy was looking down shyly.

"It's no big deal. It's just what I do."

"So you guessed my name?"

"I must have. Sometimes I don't know where my knowledge comes from."

"That's fascinating."

"By the way, I'm Amy."

"Well, it was nice meeting you," Leslie said smiling. "I'm sure we'll run into each other again sometime."

Leslie was about to continue with her shopping when she noticed Amy looking at her strangely. Her eyes were wide open and, although she seemed to be staring directly at her, she suddenly had a vacant expression, like a blind person.

"Are you all right?"

Amy didn't answer and Leslie had to ask again.

"Oh, I'm fine. Sorry, but I was just suddenly aware of something. There's a very strong aura coming from you and I'm afraid it's not a very positive one."

"Really," Leslie said somewhat sarcastically.

"If you don't want to hear about it, I won't tell you. Some people get offended when I do unsolicited readings."

"Be my guest," Leslie said.

"It's a very strong aura—extremely strong. Unfortunately, I see a lot of trauma and tension in your life. You're married, aren't you?"

"Yes," Leslie said. She was starting to think that Amy might be insane.

"Your husband's name is Daniel, right? No. I'm sorry, it's Dabney. No, that's not right either. It's David. His name is David, right?"

"How did you know that?"

"Can I see your palm?"

Leslie hesitated, then held out her hand. Amy held it loosely by the wrist.

"Just as I thought. The tension has to do with you and your husband. Your marriage has been in trouble lately and, unfortunately, things are going to get worse. He's doing something to hurt you—he's keeping a secret from you."

"What type of secret?" After Amy had guessed David's name Leslie had become more interested.

"I'm not sure, but it's something bad, I know that. And when you find out it's going to hurt you a great deal. You should confront him about it right away."

"Confront him about what?"

"About whatever he's doing to deceive you."

"This is all very interesting, but—"

"Believe me. If you wait any longer it's going to be very bad for you. Confront him about it tonight and then leave him as soon as possible."

"You're telling me to leave my husband?"

"Yes. Before it's too late."

Now Leslie was convinced that there was something seriously wrong with this woman. A few people shopping in the aisle were looking nervously in Amy's direction. Leslie dismissed Amy with a quick "Thank you," and rolled her wagon toward the check-out counter. She considered leaving the wagon filled with food in the store and taking a cab home. She was afraid that Amy would continue to harass her while she was on line, or try to follow her out of the supermarket. But when she looked back toward the canned-food aisle Amy was gone.

Leslie tried to put the entire incident out of her

mind, but on her way home she started to feel nervous. She thought about all of her problems with David and about how strange he'd been acting lately and about the blank cassette arriving; she wondered if it could all somehow be related.

Leslie had a feeling Amy was following her and she kept looking back over her shoulder as she walked along Seventy-ninth Street.

Nine

HE WAS CALLED Billy Balls for a reason. Changing for gym class in high school one day, his nuts looked like two paperweights hanging in his underwear. A guy from the football team yelled out "Hey everybody, check out Billy Balls," and from then on that's all anybody ever called him.

But Joey knew Billy long before he got the last name Balls. The DiStefanos lived in the house next door to the DePinos on Albany Avenue in Brooklyn. Billy and Joey had known each other since their mothers pushed them in their strollers side by side along Flatbush Avenue. They were in all the same classes at P.S. 119, and they went to Huddie Junior High and Midwood High together. When they were kids, they used to play Whiffle ball in Billy's driveway and hang out in front of Rocco's Pizzeria on Avenue J. When Joey was eight years old his father started taking him to the track on weekends and sometimes Billy came along. They usually went to Aqueduct or Belmont or, on summer nights, to Roosevelt Raceway on Long Island for the trotters. When they were eleven years old they were already placing their own bets. But from the beginning Joey was always much more of a gambler than Billy. Billy's thing was getting laid.

Sometimes Joey wondered if it was because Billy's balls were so big that he always had such a big sex drive. When he was eleven years old, when most kids were still waiting for their first pubes to grow in, Billy was already doing it with Linda Gianetti, the sixth-grade slut. He always had the best clothes—Sergio Valente jeans, tank tops, gold rope chains. In high school, he saved up for the down payment on a red Camaro and sat in it every afternoon in front of the main entrance to Midwood High School on Bedford Avenue, with all the girls gathering around him. Even when Joey had all his hair, he was never as good-looking as Billy. Joey was already spending most of his nights at the OTB on East Sixteenth Street, but sometimes Billy would invite Joey out with him and his current girlfriend and one of her friends, and they'd wind up parked on some dark street in Canarsie or near Marine Park. If it wasn't for Billy, Joey would have had to go to a hooker in Coney Island to lose his virginity, like every other kid in the neighborhood.

Then the accident happened. It was the night of high-school graduation and Billy was out with Cindi Badamo, the best-looking girl in school, coming back from a bar in Bay Ridge. Rumor had it that Cindi was giving Billy head while he was driving, when somehow he lost control of the wheel going around a bend on Kings Highway and the car crashed into a tree. The back of Cindi's head hit the steering wheel, breaking her neck, and she died later that night in the hospital. Billy was in a coma for two weeks. His mother and grandmother stayed by his bed twenty-four hours a day, praying to Jesus, and then, like a miracle, Billy woke up. He didn't remember anything about the accident and he'd forgotten a lot of other things too. The doctors said that he'd eventually recover completely, but he was never really the same.

Besides talking a lot slower, Billy always seemed distracted, fading out in the middle of conversations, and he had a short temper, snapping at people for no reason. He didn't smile or laugh as much as he used to and, sometimes, he was so depressed he didn't leave his house for days. Gradually, he started to lose his looks— gaining weight and not caring how he dressed. He grew a mustache, then a goatee, and finally a full beard. The only thing that didn't change about Billy was his need to get laid. It wasn't as easy for him to meet women, since most women realized right away that there was something screwed up about him, but some women— usually the dumber ones—still went out with him. And when he didn't have a date he was in Manhattan, going to the brothels in the East Twenties or cruising the West Side Highway for prostitutes. He'd told Joey that he'd named his cock "Super Dick" because of its inhuman ability to stay hard after he came. Joey said some day he was going to call somebody in *The Guinness Book of World Records* to do a story about him.

After Billy had recovered from his accident, Joey got him a job at the paint store where he was working. Billy was in on the paint-stealing scam and it was Billy who arranged to have the hookers in the room during the weekend trips down to Atlantic City. Although Billy sometimes wasn't a lot of fun to be around, Joey always stayed loyal to him.

Then Billy started dating a girl named Karen. Every day he came to work with a new story about how horny and wild she was in bed and all the guys at the paint store would gather around to listen. Joey had never known Billy to lie about a girl, but he wasn't sure whether Karen really existed. It wasn't like Billy to date a girl and never be seen with her, and since it was less than six months since he'd come out of the coma, Joey thought something screwy could be going on in Billy's head. Then, one hot, muggy day near the end of August, Billy came back to the paint store after his lunch break and announced that Karen wanted to take on a lot of guys at once, was anybody interested. Maybe it was because it was one of the hottest days of the year, but Billy's offer instantly turned all the guys into a pack of horny animals. The boss was out sick, which made the idea even more appealing, so nine guys loaded onto the paint truck, screaming for Billy to get them laid. Joey got on the truck too. He still wasn't sure whether Karen really existed, but if she did, he wanted to get laid just as badly as everyone else.

Karen didn't live far from the paint store. Billy drove the truck to one of the semi-detached brick houses off Utica Avenue. When he parked the car, he told everyone to sneak out quietly and hide while he rang the doorbell. No one thought of asking Billy why they needed to hide if Karen really wanted to have sex with a lot of guys, or if they did think of it no one cared enough to say anything. Giggling, some guys hid behind the bushes, others behind a parked car. When everyone was as quiet as they were going to get, Billy rang the bell. When the door opened, everyone crowded into the house, screaming and laughing.

Joey couldn't see or hear Karen. He was one of the last guys inside and with the all the noise and confusion he couldn't tell what was going on. Then everyone started going up the narrow stairwell and Joey followed. On the second floor, the crowd moved slowly into a room at the end of the hallway. Joey still didn't know what was going on and everyone was laughing like it was a big party. Then, when Joey came into the room, he saw Karen for the first time.

She was a big girl with long curly red hair. She was sitting on the bed and Billy was pulling at her white blouse, trying to get her to take it off. She didn't look very happy. She was crying as she kept trying to push Billy and the other guys away. Then something snapped in Billy. He pulled the blouse up over Karen's head, and pushed her hard onto the bed. She was saying, "No, no," but no one was paying any attention to her. The way she sounded, Joey realized that there was something wrong with her, like she might be retarded. Billy told two guys to hold her down and then he took off his pants, exposing his huge balls. Guys yelled out "Hey, Billy Balls!" and "Go for it, Billy Balls!" and other cheers to egg him on. Just about everybody was laughing.

While Billy was thrusting into Karen the cheering got even louder. Everything had happened so quickly that it took Joey a while to realize what was happening. At first, he was so caught up in it all that he was cheering himself. But after Billy got on and he saw that poor girl crying, he knew that what was happening was wrong. He had a feeling that a few other guys in the room—definitely Stevey and Chris—were feeling bad too, but no one was doing anything to stop it. Joey wanted to say something, but he knew it would come back to haunt him. The guys at the paint store were his best friends, the only friends he had, and some of them were in on the paint-stealing scam. What if they all got together and decided they wanted to cut Joey out of the deal? There wouldn't be anything he could do and he couldn't lose out on the thousands of dollars he was making.

But despite this, Joey was still going to speak up. He

saw himself as the big hero, the girl's parents having him over for dinner to thank him. But it was a few minutes later and the next guy was humping the retarded girl and Joey was still standing there, staring. Every time he wanted to move or say something a voice, another part of him, told him to stand still. The girl had already been raped by two people and he hadn't done anything to stop it. What would happen if he tried to break it up or he ran to a phone to tell the cops? Eventually, it would come out that he had been in on it from the beginning, that he had been as much for the idea as anybody else when he got on the truck, and that he had stood by the whole time without doing anything. There had been a story in the news lately about a bunch of black guys in Harlem who gang raped a woman and all the guys went to jail. Joey knew how easily he could wind up in jail now too.

He watched guy after guy mount the retarded girl— even Stevey and Chris took their turns. Now he knew she was retarded because one time when she tried to scream Billy stuffed his rolled up T-shirt into her mouth and yelled, "Shut up, you fuckin' retard!" Time must have gone by faster than Joey thought because when he looked at the clock on the dresser he was shocked to see that an hour had passed. Someone shouted that it was Joey's turn and Joey said he wasn't in the mood. Kevin Miller asked him "Why not?" and Joey said "I'm just not in the mood." A couple of guys called him "Faggot" and "Homo," then Billy stood up for him and said, "Hey, if he doesn't want to do it, he doesn't gotta do it. Leave the guy alone."

Joey was glad that Billy had stood up for him, but it didn't help him forget what Billy was doing. He couldn't believe this was the kid he grew up with, the kid Billy's mother used to brag about being so smart and good-looking. After Billy and a couple of other guys mounted the girl for their sloppy seconds—Billy made a loud, howling noise when he came—the guys started to leave. Before Billy left, Joey saw him take the sock out of the girl's mouth and asked her if she wanted a drink of water. The girl didn't answer. She looked like she was dead, with her eyes wide open, staring at the ceiling, but Joey knew she wasn't because her chest was moving.

On the way back to the paint store nobody was talking much. It reminded Joey of being in a bar near closing time, when everybody's drunk and tired and just wants a soft place to pass out.

That night in bed, Joey was expecting the doorbell or the phone to ring and he imagined a police officer saying, "You wanna come down to the station with us and answer a few questions?" He kept having to get up to piss.

Billy had promised the guys that there was no way in the world Karen would tell. He insisted that she was into having sex with a lot of guys at once, that she just fought back because that made it more exciting for her, and he even said that she might want to do it again some time. Arriving for work the next day, Joey wasn't sure how the guys would treat him. Surprisingly, everyone acted like nothing had ever happened. There was the usual joke cracking and talk about what an asshole the boss was and Kevin Miller even asked Joey if he wanted to go into the city with him and a bunch of other guys on Friday night—like less than twenty-four hours ago he wasn't calling him a faggot for not joining in on a gang rape.

As days passed, it seemed that Billy had been right about Karen. She didn't say a word to the police. Joey thought that Billy might have threatened her, and made her afraid to tell. But being gang-banged had to have a strong effect on a girl, Joey figured, especially a retarded girl, and she might have even decided that the whole thing was somehow her fault.

Gradually, Joey started to forget about it too. Billy said he had stopped going out with the girl, so what was the point in doing anything now? Besides, he was having so much fun gambling with the money from the stolen paint that nothing else seemed to matter. His mind was filled with thoughts of racetracks and casinos, horses and blackjack, and there was no room to feel bad about something he hadn't even done.

After Mario Cantello was released from prison and the paint stealing scam was busted, Joey started seeing less and less of Billy. Billy was one of the guys who continued to work for Cantello while Joey drifted around for a few years, living in his apartment in Sheepshead Bay, then moving into Manhattan after he married Maureen. Joey still spoke to Billy on the phone, especially during football season when they'd call each other on Sunday afternoons to talk about the bets they'd made on the games. Through other people from the neighborhood that he ran into or spoke to on the phone, Joey knew that Billy's drinking was getting out of control. He was getting ripped every night, starting bar fights, and sleeping with hookers. His mother had met some guy and she moved out into an apartment so now Billy had the house on Albany Avenue all to himself. The mortgage was paid off so all he had to do was pay the bills. He quit working for Cantello and just had a part-time job at a bicycle store. He didn't seem like the happiest guy in the world, but Joey was just glad he didn't hear any more stories about retarded girls.

* * *

Although he hadn't spoken to Billy since Super Bowl Sunday, and before that they hadn't spoken for more than a year, Joey was certain that Billy would help him out. Just like Joey had stood by Billy after his accident, he knew that Billy would stand by him now. It's just the way things were with old friends.

From the Fourteenth Street subway station, Joey called Billy. The call had woken him up and Billy said he had gotten shit-faced last night and his head felt like it was about to fall off, but when Joey said he needed to talk to him right away about something important—in person—Billy told him to come right over. But he told him to call him from the corner before he came because he was so tired he might not hear the doorbell.

When Joey got out of the IRT train subway station at the junction of Flatbush and Nostrand Avenues he had the same feeling of going into the past that he always felt. His life in Manhattan was so different from his old life in Brooklyn that it was hard for him to believe that Manhattan and Brooklyn were on the same planet. Although only a few stores were still there from the time he was growing up, every street corner and storefront reminded him of something that had happened when he was a kid. He could almost see himself walking with his dad in the snow to get the newspaper, or walking home from school with a bunch of his friends.

The biggest change between now and when Joey was a kid was the amount of black people in the neighborhood. When he was growing up, the neighborhood was almost all white, but now, as he walked up Flatbush Avenue, every face he saw was black. Joey had nothing against black people, he just missed his old neighborhood, the way it used to be. He imagined that the black kids living here today would feel the same way if they came back twenty years later and saw that the Koreans or some other group had taken over.

The last time Joey had been back to his old neighborhood was about eight years ago. Except for all the black kids, standing on the street corners, listening to their loud rap music, things looked almost exactly the same. Rocco's Pizzeria was still on Avenue J and Joey had memories of hanging out on the street corners with a bunch of other guys, drinking beer out of paper bags, and playing pool and poker with the old men at the Knights of Columbus. There were still kids hanging out on the street corners, but they were all black, and they looked at Joey angrily and suspiciously as he passed by.

On Albany Avenue, Joey stopped in front of his old house. It was a narrow two-story building with the same ugly pale-green shingles that his father had put on in 1967. Joey started thinking about his father, imagining him mowing the tiny square of lawn in front of the house with the rusty manual lawn mower and a thick cigar hanging out of his mouth. Then he imagined seeing his mother's head poking out of the window and her hoarse smoker's voice screaming "Carmine, time for dinner!" Suddenly, Joey's happy memories were replaced with images of his parents in the cancer ward at Sloan-Kettering in Manhattan. Three weeks after his mother was diagnosed with lung cancer his father found out he had cancer in his liver. His father out-lived his mother though, by two and a half months. Joey remembered how he'd dumped his father's ashes onto the paddock at Aqueduct, and how Billy had come with him. Life was hard after that. Joey was fifteen and he had to leave the neighborhood and all his friends and go live with his aunt in Mill Basin.

A black kid, about ten years old, was standing in the

driveway, staring at Joey. Joey didn't know how long the kid had been there, but it seemed like a long time. Joey felt embarrassed, like he had been caught trespassing, and he continued up the block to Billy's house. It looked exactly the same as Joey's old house except it had been painted brown. After he walked up the five-step brick stoop and rang the bell, Joey looked behind him and saw that the little black kid had moved on to the sidewalk and was still staring at him. Billy didn't answer the door right away and Joey remembered that he had wanted him to call first from the corner. He was on his way down the stoop when the door opened. Billy looked worse than Joey had ever seen him. He seemed to have aged ten years, losing most of his hair and putting on a gut. His beard was long and dirty, like there might be food caught in it. It was hard to believe that he was the same guy who'd sat in his Camaro in front of Midwood High School with his wavy black hair and cool shades. He was naked except for a towel around his waist and, although the sun was hidden behind clouds, he was squinting like he was staring at bright sunshine.

"Hey, Joey," he said, then he became distracted, noticing the little black kid. "What the fuck are you looking at?" he yelled. "Get the fuck off my property before I get out my gun. You think I'm kiddin' you?"

The black kid waited a few seconds then, with no change of expression, back-stepped toward his house.

When Joey was inside Billy said, "The fuckin' niggers in this neighborhood are driving me crazy. They're like fucking cockroaches. You see one then the next day boom—millions of 'em. What the fuck happened to you?"

Joey didn't know what Billy was talking about for a second, then he remembered about the stitches and the bruises on his face. He also realized that this was probably why the black kid had been staring at him.

"It has to do with why I needed to talk to you," Joey said. "Can we sit down?"

Billy led Joey into the kitchen, where he put out the only food he had—a two-liter bottle of Pepsi and a bag of stale Cheetos. There was a pile of dishes in the sink, garbage overflowing in the corner, and the whole place smelled like sour milk. Joey explained how he'd been on a long losing streak and how he'd almost bailed out at the Meadowlands, but how now he'd dug an even bigger hole for himself. Then he talked about how he was fired from his job and about all the money he owed and how he'd had to borrow from a Puerto Rican loan shark and how Carlos' boys had pushed him around last night. The whole time Billy didn't seem to be listening to Joey although he kept saying things like "Yeah" or "No shit" or "You're kiddin' me." He was looking all over the room, and sometimes he just rested his forehead in his open palms and stared down at the table. Joey didn't know if Billy was acting this way because of his hangover or if it had something to do with the car accident. But when Joey finished talking Billy seemed to have heard everything because he said:

"You know you can always count on me, man. The thing is I'm flat fuckin' broke. I had to take my car in last week, it's gonna run me two hundred bucks to fix something in the headlights and I don't even got that. And Dominic, my boss at the bike store, says he might not need me no more after next month. Forget about ten thousand or whatever the fuck amount of money you need."

"I know you don't have that kind of money," Joey said, "and I'm not asking for it." Joey paused, thinking how he wanted to say it. "The idea I have is gonna sound crazy to you, but you know I'm not crazy, right? You know I'm a normal guy and I wouldn't even say something crazy unless I was absolutely sure that there was nothing crazy about it."

"Yeah," Billy said, staring off again.

Joey waited for Billy to look at him and then he said, "I want to kidnap somebody."

Billy stared at Joey with a dazed look and Joey wasn't sure whether he had heard him. He was about to repeat himself when Billy said, "That's a joke, right?"

"Look at this face," Joey said seriously. "Does it look like it's joking?"

"You're fucking crazy," Billy said. "Hello? Is there anybody in there?"

"I'm serious," Joey said. "If there was some other way, believe me, I'd do it. But I thought of everything, even robbing my old boss, and this is the only way I can come up with the money. I know it doesn't sound like the most normal thing in the world to be talking about, but it beats the hell out of getting my head bashed in on the sidewalk."

"So what are you gonna do, just pick up some stranger on the street and ask for a million dollars to give him back?"

"Not a stranger, somebody I know—a little girl. And I didn't think about how I'm gonna do it yet or how much money I'm gonna ask for. I just came up with the idea this morning."

Billy rested his elbows on the table and started scratching his scalp.

"Look, I got really ripped last night and I'm really not in the mood for this bullshit right now."

"I'm only here for one reason, because I need you,"

Joey said. "Who the fuck else would I turn to? This girl I want to kidnap, she's the daughter of one of Maureen's friends. She's like ten years old and she knows me. I can't do this alone. I'm gonna need somebody to help me get her and then I need a place to keep her, just for a day or two. Fuck, it may even be less than that. I'm telling you, these people, her parents, are so in love with this kid its unbelievable. As soon as they find out she's missing they'll probably pay any amount to get her back."

Billy shook his head slowly, smiling like he was telling some joke to himself, then he went over to the kitchen sink. He moved the dirty plates from on top of the pile to the counter and then bent over the running faucet and splashed water against his face. He stood up and wiped his face and beard dry with a dirty dish towel and then he used the towel to wipe off his bald head.

He said, "When you called me before I knew it had something to do with gambling. I thought you wanted to go down to A.C. for a while, play some blackjack, fuck some broads, like the good old days. But now you come in and hit me with this crazy kidnapping idea with your face bandaged up and all these crazy stories. I think I just wanna get back into bed and go to sleep."

"You said you need money, right?"

Billy stared at Joey, his mouth halfway open. He never had that dumb, lost look before the accident, Joey thought. Billy said, "So?"

"So," Joey said. "So maybe this is like a blessing for you that I called this morning. I mean there's gonna be money in this for you too. This guy, the girl's father, is fucking loaded. He's an advertising prick, lives in this fancy doorman building on the Upper East Side. I figure he's got at least a couple hundred grand stashed away, so why not ask for a cool fifty? That means twenty-five a piece and you don't have to do anything for it. Just keep a little girl in your basement for a day, two days tops."

Billy still had his mouth half-open and his eyes had crossed as if he were staring at the tip of his nose. Then, as if some loose wire snapped back into place in his brain, his eyes refocussed and he almost looked normal again. He said, "Tell me the whole story again from the top. Who's the little girl?"

Ten

DAVID HAD NEVER run around the Jackie Onassis Reservoir more than twice, but today he decided to run a third lap to burn off his excess stress. Rounding along the graveled path, David increased his speed, pumping his arms furiously so that his fists were at the level of his face. He weaved in and out of joggers, occasionally bumping into people, hearing "Watch it," or "Asshole" as he ran past. He felt light-headed, runner's high setting in, and he unzipped his windbreaker, letting the freezing air cool his sweaty chest.

In the distance, about a hundred yards ahead, he focussed on a lamppost. Closer to him, about fifty yards away, he spotted a heavyset man wearing a bulky down winter jacket, jogging at very slow pace. David told himself that if he beat the fat man to the lamppost then Amy Lee would leave his life forever. Of course David didn't think there was a chance in the world he couldn't beat the man there—that was the whole point.

David increased his speed and seemed to be gaining on the man with every stride. After only several seconds, he was already within about twenty yards of the man and the "finish line" was still about fifty yards away. Then, as if he knew that he was in a race, the man started sprinting. David started to speed up too, almost knocking down an old woman who was walking in the other direction. But the fat man was much faster and he beat David to the lamppost by several strides.

David took the defeat as a message from Satan. He stopped running, suddenly exhausted, fearing that he would pass out. The scene was so vivid—the EMS workers arriving, carrying his body off on a stretcher as a crowd looked on. He stopped walking and tried to catch his breath, leaning with his open hands against the fence between the path and the reservoir.

* * *

Less than twenty-four hours earlier, David had his latest "Amy scare." Saturday morning he had gone into the office to catch up on some work. It was relaxing to be at the office when it was empty and there were no distractions. When he arrived back in his apartment, at around three in the afternoon, he was confronted by the odor of cigarette smoke. He traced the fumes to the bedroom where Leslie was sitting Indian-style on the bed with a plate covered with cigarette butts resting next to her. Her latest cigarette was half-smoked, between her middle and index fingers.

"What's wrong?" David asked.

Suddenly, he had remembered that her father had undergone a coronary bypass operation last year. He wondered if someone had died.

"Don't worry," Leslie said, recognizing David's urgent tone. "I just felt like smoking a couple of cigarettes. Is there something wrong with that?"

"But you don't smoke," David said.

Leslie turned off the TV with the remote control, then put out the rest of her cigarette on the plate.

"I need to talk to you about something that happened today."

Now David wondered if the smoking had something to do with Amy Lee. David decided to play it cool, not give anything away.

"Let's open some windows in here," David said, "air this place out."

"Didn't you hear what I said?" Leslie said. "I want to talk to you about something and it's very important to me."

"Talk," David said, opening the window, letting the distant sounds of traffic and sirens into the apartment. "Who's stopping you?"

"Is something wrong?"

"Wrong?" David said. "Why would something be wrong?"

"You seem upset about something."

"It's the cigarette smoke," David said, trying too hard not to sound aggravated. "You know how allergic I get to it. I don't understand why you'd start smoking. Do you want to die of cancer?"

"Did something happen at work?"

"No," David said almost yelling. He pulled the cord on the Venetian blinds too hard and the blind popped out of its bracket. David paused, trying to get a hold of himself. "It's the smoke," he said definitively. "I hate smoke."

"Remember I told you I met that Chinese woman at Macy's the other day?"

Still facing the window, David closed his eyes.

"Chinese woman?"

"You remember—the one who was telling me all about her boyfriend problems?"

David cringed.

"Oh, *her*."

"You wouldn't believe it—I ran into her in Gristede's today."

"Is that right?"

"Don't you think that it was a big coincidence? At first I didn't give it much thought, but then I thought, in New York what are the odds? It made me wonder, especially after she started talking to me about how she was a psychic and she knew all this stuff about us."

"Us?"

"She knew my name—even though I'm almost positive I never told her—and she knew your name too. Get this—she said my aura gave it away. Then she told me how there's a lot of trauma and tension in my life and how you're doing something to hurt me. She said you're keeping some secret from me and I have to confront you about it."

David was trying to put the blind back into its bracket, but he fumbled again and the blind crashed onto the floor.

"God damn it. I hate these fucking things."

"Are you paying attention to me?"

"Yes," he said, still facing the window.

"So what do you think? Don't you think it's very strange?"

"I don't think it's *so* strange."

"What do you mean? I think the woman might be totally bonkers. I was afraid she was going to try to follow me home."

"I doubt she'd do that."

"Really? And what makes you so sure?"

"Because, like you just said, she's probably—I mean it sounds like she's probably crazy. I bet she talks to people in supermarkets and department stores all the time."

"But she knew our names. She seemed to know all about us. I can't believe you're not more upset about this."

David finally snapped the blind back into place. He turned back toward Leslie.

"There. That shouldn't fall down again. You know, we should really get these blinds replaced. How long have we had them now?"

"I can still see her eyes," Leslie said. "She had these crazy eyes. I don't think she blinked one time."

"Forget about it," David said. "It's over."

"What about those things she said?"

"You know that psychic stuff is all a load of bullshit. She probably took a couple of lucky guesses. David isn't exactly the most exotic name in the world you know. If you didn't tell her she was right she probably would have said "Bob" and "Jim" and "Harry" and every other name until she got it right. It's certainly not something that's worth getting cancer over. And do me a favor—if you're going to smoke again, do it on the terrace."

David left the bedroom. From the hallway he announced that he was going to go down to the lobby to pick up the mail. Waiting for the elevator, he leaned against the wall, trying to get a hold of himself. He was sweating so much he could smell his own body odor. Under the circumstances, he thought he had handled himself fairly well, but maybe Leslie was just pretending she didn't know about the affair. Maybe she just wanted to make him admit it.

In the lobby, the doorman said something to David. He was so distracted he had to ask him to repeat himself.

"There's a letter here for your wife."

"A letter?"

The doorman, the young black guy who only worked on weekends, was holding a plain white envelope. LESLIE was written across the front of it in black magic marker.

"Who dropped this off?"

"A woman."

"When?"

"Half hour ago."

"What did she look like?"

"Chinese. Thin."

David went to the back of the lobby, away from the elevators, and opened the envelope. Inside was a piece of notebook paper, torn out with a frazzled edge. He read the note several times, although there was nothing very complex about it.

IT'S BEEN A PLEASURE FUCKING YOUR HUSBAND
LOVE, YOUR FAVORITE PSYCHIC

David remained in the corner, trying to ward off another panic attack. He didn't understand what he had done to deserve such torture. He decided that it was ridiculous to go on like this. Eventually, Leslie would find out and it would be better if she heard it from him directly. He ripped the note into the smallest pieces possible and stuffed the scraps into his back pocket. He would tell Leslie everything. Whatever happened afterwards had to be better than this.

Back in the apartment, Leslie was pouring herself a glass of diet soda when David came in. He said, "I have to talk to you about something. Something very important."

"What?" Leslie said.

Somewhere between his brain and his lips David's courage died. He was thinking about how devastated he was at twelve years old to find out that his parents were divorcing. At ten it would probably have an even worse effect on Jessica. She was living such a happy life now it seemed crazy to ruin it all.

"I love you," David said seriously.

Leslie seemed confused, then she smiled.

"I love you, too."

David, Leslie and Jessica had been planning to sit home all night and watch a video on TV. Usually, David would go to Blockbuster on Second Avenue by himself, but tonight he insisted that the whole family go together. Although he had no plan for what he would do if Amy approached them on the street, he was afraid that she would call the apartment as soon as he was gone.

When they came back from the video store, the phone was ringing. David rushed to answer it, but the caller had already hung up. Thinking fast, he went to the answering machine in his study and saw the number 3 flashing. He told Leslie that he needed to make an important call to a client and played the messages at a low volume. Sure enough, Amy had left three messages. In the first message she said, "Hi, David, it's Amy. Call me." In the second message, sounding sexier, she said, "Hi, David, I'm just lying here in bed thinking about you. I miss you. Call me." Then in the third message, she sang, *"I just called to say I love you..."* and then she said, "Please give me a call, David."

Breathing heavily, David called Information and asked for Amy's home telephone number. She wasn't listed. He was worried for a moment, then he had a brainstorm. He dialed *69, the telephone company's call-return feature. On the third ring, Amy answered.

David, speaking in a whisper, told Amy that he cared about her very much, but that trying to break up his family was not the way to start their lives together. He told her that he was planning to leave Leslie, but he couldn't do it so suddenly. He pleaded for her to back off for at least another week. Amy said she had waited long enough and that she was tired of listening to his lies. If David didn't tell Leslie that he was in love with another woman right now, Amy was going to come over and tell her herself. There was a knock on David's office door. It was Jessica, asking when David was going to be off the phone. David said he wouldn't be more than a few minutes longer. In a hushed voice, he begged Amy to give him until Monday evening. He told her that he had strong feelings for her too and that if she really felt the same way she would give him some time. This seemed to have an effect on Amy. After a long silence, she said that she would leave him alone until Monday, but warned that she wouldn't wait any longer. Then she said that she missed David and wished him a good night.

David might have paid attention to a scene or two from the movie—the latest Disney comedy. As Jessica and Leslie watched engrossed, eating frozen yogurt, David wondered what he would do after Monday. All he had done was buy a little more time—two more days. Nothing had been solved. If anything, things had gotten worse. He cursed himself for telling Amy that he had "strong feelings" for her. What if she had been taping the conversation and played it for Leslie along with the other tape? Then, looking at Jessica sitting happily, Indian-style in front of the television, David remembered how much he had to lose.

Halfway through the movie, Leslie paused the film and said she had to go to the bathroom.

"Mom's sick," Jessica said.

"Sick?" David said, his mind still elsewhere.

"She said she has a stomach virus. She's been throwing up all week, but I don't believe her."

"Why don't you believe her?"

"I think there's something else wrong with her."

When Leslie returned a few minutes later David asked her if everything was all right.

"Of course," she said. "Why wouldn't it be?"

Now David was convinced that Leslie knew. Even if she didn't know it consciously, her unconscious mind was aware of it, which explained her weak stomach.

Later, as Leslie was getting into her nightgown, David noticed that the fat on her thighs was disappearing and that her stomach looked flatter. She looked as if she had lost ten pounds. Maybe getting this stomach virus wasn't such a bad thing.

"What are you doing?"

David continued to kiss Leslie's neck, biting down with his teeth.

Afterwards, when they were lying next to each other in the dark, Leslie asked David what he was thinking about.

David was convinced that she knew.

* * *

David decided not to let Amy ruin his Sunday. In the afternoon, after he came back from running, Leslie wanted to stay home and cook a nice dinner and David took Jessica to the Museum of Natural History. She had outgrown her obsession with dinosaurs a few years ago and was now fascinated by the ecosystem exhibits. She seemed to know more about global warming than many meteorologists and her big dream in life was to some day become the weather woman on the Channel Two News.

David was extremely proud of Jessica. Although he had always wanted a son and was admittedly disappointed when Leslie's sonogram had not shown a penis, he had grown so fond of Jessica that he didn't want to have any other children. Leslie agreed and, shortly after Jessica was born, had gone for the operation to have her tubes tied.

Jessica led David through the museum as if it were her private palace. Then they went to Columbus Avenue for a pizza lunch and they spent the rest of the afternoon at the Hayden Planetarium. By the time they arrived back at their apartment, at around five o'clock, David had had such a good time that he'd forgotten that tomorrow was Monday and that Amy Lee was even alive.

Later, Leslie helped Jessica with her homework and David tried to absorb himself in a proposal he was working on for a client. The client, an Italian jewelry manufacturer, had previously been advertising only in print media, and now wanted to begin an ad campaign for television. David was making his proposal based on demographics he had compiled, along with a suggested budget. It had the potential to turn into a multi-million dollar project, but David could hardly concentrate on his work. He couldn't seem to find a comfortable position in his swivel chair and he kept having to scroll back on his PC to re-read what he had just written.

When he came into the bedroom, Leslie was still awake, turning pages of *Allure* magazine. She said she wasn't feeling well and didn't think she could make love, which was fine with David. He had trouble falling asleep and finally left the bedroom and went into the living room to watch TV. An infomercial on a new stomach exerciser bored him to sleep. It seemed like only a few minutes later he was awake—a line of morning sunshine coming through the Venetian blinds was stinging his eyes. It felt like the morning of his execution. He was too exhausted to move and yet his heart was pounding as if he had drunk five mugs of coffee.

Otherwise, it was a typical Monday morning at home. Leslie was busy getting Jessica ready for school and a pot of coffee was waiting for David. Already wearing her mink coat, Leslie came into the kitchen and said, "It's going to snow today."

"How much?"

"They say ten inches. It depends on how the storm moves up the coast."

"It's probably just hype. Those weathermen are all full of shit."

David felt like his brain was working on automatic, having a conversation that everybody has when a snowstorm is predicted. It occurred to him that he didn't even have to be here. Another man or a robot could take his place and fill in the role of husband and father very easily.

Jessica was in a great mood, extremely excited about the upcoming storm.

"I saw the satellite pictures on TV. The storm is going to hug the coast. It's going to be the biggest blizzard in New York City history!"

"You think so?" David asked with feigned interest.

"Yes," Jessica said confidently. "I should be on the TV doing all the weather forecasts."

"You will some day, pumpkin," David assured her.

When Jessica was ready for school, David felt a

sudden rush of loss, as if he was seeing her for the last time. As he kissed her on the top of her head and then hugged her goodbye, he tried to memorize exactly what his happy daughter was like, knowing that she might never be this way again. Then he kissed Leslie goodbye, praying that she would be able to forgive him.

As usual, David took a cab to work. When he got out in front of his office building the first flurries were falling. Looking up at the swirling flakes, he prayed again for a miracle.

David expected Amy to be waiting for him in his office. She wasn't there, but he knew this wasn't exactly cause for celebration. Knowing her, she was probably timing her appearance to make him as stressed-out as possible. He tried to work on his presentation, but anxious thoughts kept intruding. He took a break, massaging another dosage of Minoxidil into his scalp, but he knew the treatments weren't working. The gene for baldness was handed down from the mother and his two uncles on his mother's side had heads like billiard balls, as did his mother's father. He imagined being bald and lonely, living by himself in some walk-up apartment building. He wondered if Jessica would even want to spend weekends with him.

During the morning staff meeting, he continued to ruminate about his uncertain future. A few people asked him whether he was feeling all right. He answered vaguely, realizing, but not really caring, how strange he sounded.

Around noon, Eric came into his office.

"Blizzard?" David said. "What blizzard?"

He swiveled in his chair and parted the blinds covering his windows. It was so white outside he could barely see Second Avenue.

"They say it's not even the main part of the storm yet," Eric said. "It's really going to kick in this afternoon and tonight."

"My daughter's a genius," David said.

"Your daughter?"

"She said this storm was gonna be huge."

"Every weather report in the city has been predicting this storm all weekend," Eric said.

"You trying to say my daughter isn't a genius?"

"I—"

"You haven't even met my daughter," David snapped. "She's the smartest kid in school. She's probably smarter than half the people in this agency."

"I'm sure she is," Eric said. "Well, it was nice chatting with you too."

"Hey, I'm sorry," David said. "Don't go."

Eric stopped near the door and turned back around. David said, "I guess I'm just a little edgy today."

"A little?" Eric said. "People are worried about you, man. Let me take a wild guess. Does this happen to have something to do with Amy Lee?"

"Lock the door."

Eric turned the lock and then David told him to sit down. David said, "She's been harassing the hell out of me and Leslie."

"Leslie knows?"

"I think she at least senses it. But it's only a matter of time till she knows for sure."

David told Eric about everything that had happened over the weekend and about Amy's ultimatum. A few times Eric interjected, but mostly he just sat quietly, occasionally shaking his head. When David was through Eric said, "This is crazy, man. You have to do something."

"Like what?"

"Threaten her back. Tell her you'll take the pictures and notes she's sent you and get her fired."

"That'll only make her angrier. I'm telling you, there are screws loose in her head. Besides, she'll never believe me because she knows all I'm worried about is Leslie finding out."

"What about making your own tape—of Amy trying to blackmail you. You can play it for Leslie and maybe she'll understand."

"Understand what? There's no nice way to tell your wife that you've been cheating on her. What'll I say, 'But she was trying to blackmail me—now do you forgive me, honey?' I'm sure that'll go over really well."

"So what are you gonna do?"

"I'll tell her that she can do whatever she wants. She wants to send letters to Leslie, call her up, follow her into a supermarket, let her do it. I'm not putting up with any more of this bullshit."

"You realize what it could be like when you go home tonight?"

"I deserve whatever I get," David said. "It's my fault for getting myself into this situation."

"Hey, that's crazy," Eric said. "You can't control people. You didn't know she'd flip out like this."

"I could've ended the whole thing sooner—before it got out of control."

"That's easy to say now."

"No," David said, shaking his head. "I definitely *let* this happen. I didn't tell you this the other day, but I definitely told her a few things she could have misunderstood."

"Like what?"

"A lot of things—what difference does it make? The point is I have to accept some responsibility now. I've been a shitty husband and a shitty father and this is my payback."

"Well, if you want some support tonight I could come home with you, or maybe the four of us could meet for dinner. I can call Debbie at work and see what she's doing—"

"I appreciate it," David said, "but I'll be able to handle it alone."

What a crock of shit, David thought after Eric left his office. There was no way he was going to be able to *handle* coming home tonight, having Leslie attack him. He saw flashes of the scene—Leslie screaming and cursing while Jessica stood by watching.If Leslie kicked him out of the apartment he realized he'd have nowhere to go. He'd probably have to move back with his mother and stepfather on Long Island, into his old room. The walls were still covered with Wacky stickers and baseball posters of Hank Aaron and Willie Mays.

David didn't answer his telephone all afternoon. Around three o'clock, there were frequent calls and he assumed it was Amy calling to find out whether he had told Leslie yet. But if Amy wanted to talk to him she'd have to show up in person. He didn't even play back his messages because the thought of hearing her voice made him nauseous.

It was ten minutes to five. If Amy was planning to show up at his office he didn't know what was taking her so long. The snow was coming down even harder now and he wondered if it was possible that she had decided not to come into work today. Or maybe she'd had a sudden change of heart—woke up and realized she was insane.

Most people in the office had left earlier in the afternoon to get a jump on the storm. As David put on his winter coat and gloves he was aware of the unusual silence. On most days, he would hear phones ringing, people talking, cars and sirens from outside. But now there was hardly any noise at all.

When he opened his office door, Amy was standing there, wearing a black wool coat and a matching hat. She said, "Are you ready to spend the rest of your life with me now?"

Eleven

LESLIE COULDN'T BELIEVE that she weighed only 109 pounds. If her scale wasn't broken it would mean that she had lost three pounds in the last two days while it felt like she had put on five. Looking at herself in the mirror on her bedroom door, she noticed how the tops of her thighs still rubbed together and how she still had that triangle of dimples on her behind. She reminded herself that this was her "thin mirror," so she probably looked even more blubbery and disgusting.

She felt the crackers she'd just stuffed into her mouth gurgling in the back of her throat and rushed into the bathroom. But just as she kneeled over the toilet bowl Jessica knocked on the door and said, "Mommy, I'm going to be late for school."

Leslie fought to keep the crackers down. It wasn't easy. She closed her eyes and pressed her lips together and concentrated on keeping her throat closed. The crackers were digesting, but she wasn't sure she was happy about this. She'd probably gain a pound from them and the scale *had* to be five pounds under. To make up for it, she'd have to skip lunch, have a salad with no dressing for dinner.

Then, as she squeezed the back of her hips and poked her thumbs into her narrow waist, she thought about Dr. Sloan, the psychiatrist her parents had made her see when she was sixteen. Dr. Sloan told her that obsessions with food and weight were often reflections of other problems at home. He had linked her anorexia as a teenager to neurosis from her mother being a Holocaust survivor. Leslie was never sure whether she believed this or not, but now she wondered if her problems with food might in some way be related to David.

When they were having sex the other night she felt like she was being attacked. At the time, she was convinced that there must be something wrong with her. She was dispassionate, neurotic, maybe even a repressed lesbian. But now she decided that she wasn't entirely to blame. David was the one who'd been acting cold and removed lately, and he wasn't at all understanding or supportive when she told him about the woman who'd been stalking her. Leslie was so angry she slammed down the toilet seat cover and flushed so hard she nearly broke off the handle.

Then, as the water swirled down the drain, she wondered if it was possible that David was having an affair. It would explain all the late nights at the office, his coldness in bed, the way he seemed distracted all the time. But David was such a lousy liar Leslie couldn't imagine him having an affair without giving himself away.

As Leslie was walking Jessica to school the first snowflakes were starting to fall.

"It's a blizzard already," Jessica said. "And this afternoon it's really gonna be coming down."

Leslie was distracted, wondering if that Chinese woman was following her again.

"Walk faster, honey," Leslie said. "You don't want to be late."

As she walked, Leslie lighted a cigarette.

* * *

"That's her—the blonde chick with the cigarette," Joey said to Billy. "The little girl's name is Jessica."

They were in Billy's LeSabre, driving slowly along East Seventy-seventh Street. Joey was hunched low in the passenger seat, peaking over the dashboard.

"She's cute," Billy said.

"Believe me, she's not your type," Joey said. "She's a rich Upper East Side type of chick. Doesn't even work. Just goes shopping and sits on her ass all day. Anyway, this is important, you have to figure out how to get the little girl into the car. Do it quick, but don't do it too fast. It's a good thing it's snowing today—maybe they'll let the kids out early. If you can't get her today, forget about it—there's always tomorrow. Whatever you do, don't do anything stupid and get caught. Are you listening to me?"

Billy was staring out the window.

"She's a rich Upper East Side type of chick."

"I'm trying to give you instructions here. Use all your energy and concentrate because we can't fuck things up. You concentrating? Now where are you gonna be in your car?"

"In front of the school."

"No, I told you, stay back by the hydrant over there. If the cops make you move, circle the block then go back or find a spot nearby. When you see her come out of school drive up to her, make sure you have your ski mask on. Tell her her mommy told you to pick her up—tell her you work for a car service. She's a smart little girl so she probably won't believe you, so you gotta be very convincing. Start naming names. Her mother's name's Leslie, remember that, and her father's David. Leslie and David Sussman."

"She's got a nice little ass."

Leslie was saying goodbye to Jessica in front of the school. Now Joey wasn't sure whether Billy was staring at Leslie or Jessica.

"Stop kidding around," Joey said. "You can't fuck this up so we better make sure you got it right. You have to tell her why her mommy wanted you to pick her up. Say her daddy was in an accident—he's at the hospital."

"Will you stop telling me what I fuckin' have to do?"

Suddenly, Billy looked like a mental patient, reminding Joey of some of the psychos he always saw at the racetrack and in the OTBs.

"All right, take it easy will ya?"

"Then stop it," Billy said. "Just stop it. Stop treating me like a fuckin' two-year-old."

Billy, breathing heavily, rested his forehead on the steering wheel. After letting him relax for a couple of seconds Joey said:

"You fuckin' crazy yelling like that? You want people to look over and see you like that? Then when they hear a little girl was kidnapped today they say 'I remember seeing this guy near the school in a light blue Buick.' You're lucky if somebody didn't take down your goddamn license plate number already."

Billy still had his forehead against the steering wheel.

"I'm sorry," he said, "all right? I'm fuckin' sorry."

Joey said, "Maybe we should just go home—wait till tomorrow."

"Fuck that shit," Billy said suddenly agitated again. "I got up at fuckin' six o'clock to pick you up today. You think I'm gettin' up at six again tomorrow? Fuck that shit. We do it today or we don't do it at all."

Looking at Billy's bloodshot eyes and the veins sticking out in his forehead, Joey wondered if maybe this kidnapping wasn't such a good idea after all.

* * *

When Leslie opened the door to her apartment and the phone was ringing she was positive it was Amy. Somehow she had gotten her phone number and now she was calling to make more psychic predictions. Leslie was going to let the answering machine pick up, but then she decided she was sick of letting some stranger intrude on her life and she answered the phone after the third ring.

"Hello, Leslie?"

It was Maureen. Leslie let out a deep breath and said, "I just walked in the door."

"I can't talk long anyway, I'm at work, but wait till you hear this—I took your advice."

Leslie had no idea what Maureen was talking about.

"Advice?"

"Remember, the other night, you told me I should try smiling at a good-looking guy? Well, I did it. I was at the emergency room at St. Vincent's Hospital. Joey was mugged—"

"Mugged?"

"It was no big deal. The other night, after we left your house. He was taking out the garbage and some homeless guy jumped him."

"Oh my God."

"He needed stitches, but he's okay now. Anyway, I was in the waiting room waiting for him to come out when I noticed this guy sitting across from me. He was tall and blond—very good-looking. I was gonna just ignore him, but then I remembered what you said, the advice you gave me, and I said to myself, 'Why not?' So I smiled at him. At first he seemed a little surprised and I felt like I'd made a big fool out of myself, but then he smiled back. Then you won't believe what happened. He got up and sat right down next to me. Before I knew it, we were having a conversation. He was so good-looking you wouldn't believe it. He had blond hair and his eyes were like Paul Newman's. He told me he was waiting for his brother who was having an asthma attack and then he asked me who I was waiting for. You know me, I usually never lie, but this time I didn't even think about it. Luckily, I wasn't wearing my wedding ring so I told him I was waiting for my uncle Joey." Maureen laughed. "So, anyway, we kept talking. He was telling me all about his job. He works in sales—corporate sales for a carpet company. Then his brother comes out and they're about to leave when this guy—his name's Pete—asks me if I want to have lunch with him on Monday. Again I couldn't believe it. I was saying to myself, 'Was it always this easy? Why didn't I just smile at gorgeous guys while I was single?' Anyway, I have a date this afternoon for lunch. So what do you think? Am I crazy or what?"

"I'm sorry," Leslie said. Her mind had been wandering.

"Going out with this guy," Maureen said. "Is it stupid or what? I mean I know it's crazy, but should I do it, I don't know, just to see what it's like?"

"Sure," Leslie said, suddenly exhausted. "You deserve to be happy."

"I have to tell you," Maureen said, "I'm really excited about it. I couldn't sleep for the past two nights and I've hardly even noticed Joey. It's so awful, but it feels so good at the same time."

"I'm very happy for you," Leslie said. "But I just walked in the door—"

"Oh, I have to go too—my boss is coming. I just wanted to thank you. You were so right about everything. If I was smart I would've listened to you a long time ago."

About twenty minutes later, after Leslie had two slices of toast and four tablespoons of cottage cheese for breakfast, she was still upset about something. She had no idea what it was, then she decided that it might have something to do with Maureen's call. Although she was glad that Maureen was looking for some alternative to her deadbeat husband, Leslie didn't necessarily want Maureen to be happy. Maureen's insecurity was something that Leslie could always count on. No matter how bad things got in Leslie's life, Maureen was always a step lower. But now, suddenly, their relationship had changed and Leslie wasn't sure how she felt about this.

Leslie spent the afternoon lying on the couch watching soap operas. The programs were interrupted now and then for reports on the snowstorm. In one of her shows, her favorite character was having heart transplant surgery and Leslie was so involved that she didn't even look out the window. When the program ended the Channel Seven anchor man came on and announced that a snow emergency was in effect in New York City. Leslie looked out at the swirling haze of white and only then realized that Jessica might have been let out of school early.

Usually, the school day ended at three o'clock and it was two now. Just to be on the safe side, Leslie called the school and a secretary answered.

"What do you mean?" Leslie said. "How come I wasn't called?"

The secretary explained that they were trying to call all the parents and notify them and she was surprised that Leslie hadn't gotten a call. Leslie remembered that she had let the machine pick up two or three times during her soap opera.

"So where's my daughter now?"

"She should still be at the school waiting. The children were let out almost an hour ago."

Now Leslie was very nervous. It wasn't like Jessica to dilly dally on her way home from school.

Leslie walked back to the school as fast as she could on the slippery, snow-covered sidewalks. She hadn't put on boots or gloves and after the ten-minute walk she could hardly feel her toes and fingers. Jessica wasn't outside the school or in the vestibule so Leslie went inside to look for her. The school was quiet and empty. Leslie went into the principal's office and was relieved to see Mrs. Johnson there, the young black woman whom she had become friendly with at a few of the school board meetings.

"As a matter of fact I *did* see Jessica, maybe about forty-five minutes ago. She said you told her it was all right if she walked home alone today. Why? She didn't come home?"

"No, and to be honest I'm getting very worried."

"Oh, I wouldn't worry. The kids were thrilled to have a half day today. I'm sure she's off having a snowball fight somewhere or she's on her way home now."

Leslie slid and stumbled back to her apartment building. The snow seemed to be coming down harder now, blowing straight into her face on Second Avenue.

She felt like she had been out walking in the snow and cold all day when the doorman told her that he hadn't seen Jessica. Leslie tried to stay calm. She told herself that Mrs Johnson was probably right—Jessica was just out playing in the snow somewhere, having a good time. But she couldn't help thinking that something terrible had happened. She remembered the way Amy had looked in the supermarket, staring at her with those eyes that never seemed to blink.

Leslie decided that she had to get a hold of herself, she was jumping to too many conclusions. Just because a woman had been harassing her, didn't mean that the woman had kidnapped her daughter. She walked back to the school, convinced that Jessica would be waiting for her. But Jessica wasn't there and, adding to Leslie's frustration, the doors to the school were locked. Leslie went to a phone booth and called David. His voice mail answered and she left a message, telling him to call her at home as soon as possible. Her doorman still hadn't seen Jessica. It was ten minutes after four. There were no messages on her answering machine and when she called David she got his voice mail again. Leslie was so frazzled she didn't even think of trying David at another number in his department.

She walked to the school and back a few more times. There had to be some reasonable explanation for this— Jessica was at a friend's house watching TV, everything would be fine.

Leslie called all of Jessica's friends, but no one knew where Jessica was. Two hours later, when it was pitch dark and the blizzard was in full-force, Leslie called the police.

Twelve

"WHAT ARE YOU thinking about?"

David had been staring out the window at the swirling snow, blowing and drifting against the buildings on Fifth Avenue.

"Nothing," he said.

"You don't have to be so shy around me."

David couldn't believe he was sitting in a cab with Amy Lee. In his office he had told her that his marriage was over, that he was ready to spend the rest of his life with her. He had realized it was a spineless, idiotic thing to do, but it was the memory of Jessica hugging him goodbye this morning that had made him chicken out. He just couldn't imagine the idea of being a weekend dad or, even worse, the possibility that Jessica might never want to see him again.

A few times during the ride Amy held David's hand. Each time David let her hold it for a while, then slowly wiggled free. Now Amy rested her open hand on David's left thigh. To David, it felt like his leg was caught in a clamp.

David knew that his only way out of this nightmare was to offer Amy a bribe. He had over twelve thousand dollars in a Citibank account that Leslie didn't have access to. He would start at five thousand dollars, then offer eight, then ten, and only go to twelve as a last resort. Any amount over that would mean making a withdrawal from a joint account and David knew he'd have a hard time explaining the missing money to Leslie.

Because of the snow, the cab couldn't turn on to Morton Street. David and Amy got out on Seventh Avenue South. The normally busy intersection was empty and eerily quiet. Under the dull light of the lampposts the snow seemed to have an orange tinge. Stepping on to the sidewalk, Amy slipped on her heels and interlocked her arm with David's. She continued to cling to David as they walked with the icy snow pelting against their faces. Her apartment building was in the middle of the block.

Amy lived in a large one-bedroom that David figured must cost her at least sixteen hundred a month. It was furnished sparsely with simple pine furniture, probably all purchased from IKEA in New Jersey. Amy excused herself to the bedroom while David sat at the kitchen table, staring at a framed poster of Monet's lily pads. It reminded him of his honeymoon with Leslie in Paris when they took the three-hour train ride to visit Monet's gardens in Giverny. He remembered standing with Leslie on the very foot bridge depicted in the painting, holding her tight, resting his chin on the back of her shoulder.

"Take off your coat," Amy said. "Stay awhile."

Amy had changed into black leggings and an oversized white T-shirt. She was barefoot and David could tell she had put on more of that annoyingly strong perfume she always wore. Her odor reminded David of the times he waited for Leslie to finish shopping in the cosmetics department at Bloomingdale's. Amy came up behind David and pulled his coat off over his shoulders.

"How about a nice hot cup of tea?"

David shook his head.

"Coffee? Hot cocoa? I'll make you a nice hot cocoa. That'll warm you up."

As Amy put up the water to boil David continued to stare at the Monet poster.

Amy said, "By the way, I already cleared out two drawers in my dresser for you. I don't know when you want to start moving your things over, but I have an extra key I'll give you tomorrow morning. Oh, and you can have the whole hall closet. I guess eventually we can start looking for a two- or three-bedroom. I don't know about you, but I'd rather live in the Village than the Upper East Side. It's a little too uptight up there for my taste. I guess we'll have to see how well you do in your divorce settlement before we decide how much we can afford. Personally, I'd rather live in a big apartment than a lavish one. The most important thing is space. Of course I didn't have any brothers or sisters, but if I did I know I wouldn't have wanted to share a room with them, so I don't see why our children would want to share a room either. We may want to consider a house, not in the suburbs, in the country somewhere. It would depend on what kind of job you can get and finding a school for your daughter—that is if you win the custody battle. Are you okay?"

David was still staring at the poster.

"How much do you want?"

"Want?" Amy said. "I don't know what you're talking about."

"Come on, you're an intelligent woman. You must

know on some level how ridiculous this all is. You know this isn't how relationships start. So I'm asking you again —how much do you want to leave me alone forever?"

Amy stared at David for a few seconds, her jaw hanging halfway open.

"This is a joke, right? You didn't really just say what I think you said."

"How about five thousand dollars?"

Amy laughed sarcastically.

"You think I want your money? I can't believe that. After all the time we've spent together I'd think you'd have a little bit more respect for me than *that*."

"We fucked a few times and that was it. I could've gotten the same thing out of a call girl and if I was smart I would've. Eight thousand dollars tomorrow morning in an envelope and let's call it quits."

The whistle on the kettle was sounding, the water starting to boil. The sound grew louder and shriller and Amy still didn't move. Finally—as if she were aware of the sound for the first time—Amy shut off the flame.

"I have an idea," Amy said, "let's pretend none of this just happened. I'll come out of the bedroom again and we can start all over."

"Ten thousand and that's my final offer."

Now Amy had that deadpan look again.

"I don't think you understand what type of woman I really am," she said. "I'm a good woman, an honest woman, and I know what I deserve. I'll tell you one thing—I'm a lot better than that haggard old wife of yours. When I'm your wife I won't sit home on a Sunday morning while you and your daughter go to the museum. I'll spend every minute of the day being the best mother and wife I can be."

"How do you know we were at the museum?"

"Give me a break," Amy said. "I have a right to spend time with my future family, don't I? And I'll tell you one thing—your daughter doesn't look like a happy little girl. I spoke to her in the ladies room and she didn't seem to like her mommy very much at all."

"How come I didn't see you there?" David asked.

"You looked right at me," Amy said, "but I can look like a totally different person with my blonde wig and sunglasses."

David wondered how many other times Amy had followed him and his family. He stood up and started putting on his coat.

"All right, twelve thousand and that's absolutely all I can afford. Take it or leave it."

"Sit down right now," Amy said.

"I'm going home to be with my family," David said. "If I were you I'd take my money and use it to pay for a good psychiatrist."

As David was unbolting the door Amy said, "Wait."

Something in the tone of Amy's voice made David turn around. She was holding a gun, aiming it directly at his face.

"Are you out of your mind?"

Amy's pocketbook was open on the table. David realized that was where the gun had come from.

"What are you doing with a gun?"

"Sit right back down in that chair," Amy said, "and take off your coat."

"What do you think's going to happen?" David said, not moving his gaze away from the gun. "You point a gun at my face and you think we can live happily ever after?"

"Sit down," Amy said impatiently. Her right arm, holding the gun, started to shake, and she grabbed the wrist with her left hand to steady it. "Sit *down*."

"Look at yourself," David said. "You're insane."

"If you don't sit the fuck down right now—"

"What? You'll shoot me?" David couldn't believe how calm he was acting. "What good will that do? You won't be able to marry me if I'm dead."

"I'll kill both of us."

"Relax, okay?"

"I'm warning you—"

"Look, just put the gun down."

"Stay back."

"Give it to me."

As David moved closer he was watching Amy's finger.

"I said keep back!"

David lunged forward. He grabbed her arm that was holding the gun with one hand and wrestled the gun free with the other. The gun fell to the floor. He pushed her back and she tripped over the leg of the table and fell backwards. He could see her eyes staring at him in horror, her mouth opening to scream. Then the back of her head hit the edge of the counter top. She fell on to the floor and lay there motionless on her side, blood leaking from her head. But David kept going. He was acting on impulse, aware of nothing except his own rage. He picked up the first object within his reach—a heavy frying pan from the stove—and swung it, as hard as he could, against her face. He hit her at least five or six more times before he realized what he was doing. Now blood was flowing freely from Amy's nose and mouth.

David couldn't breathe. His pulse was pounding so fast he thought he was going to have a stroke or a seizure. He couldn't believe what he'd done. He'd never hit anyone before or been in a fight. He started crying—tears streaming down his cheeks. He squeezed his eyes closed, hoping this was all a nightmare. Then he opened his eyes and saw Amy's curled up body on the floor. The blood was flowing faster.

David took a step toward the telephone then froze. His mind was spinning.

Ambulance equals police, equals life in prison, equals Leslie finding out about the affair, equals divorce, equals never seeing Jessica again.

He leaned over with his hands on his knees, taking slow, deep breaths, trying to calm himself. Then he grabbed a dish towel and started wiping things off. Luckily, he hadn't left the kitchen. He wiped down the whole table and the chair he'd been sitting on, and he wiped off the gun, replacing it on the floor. Then he wiped off the frying pan, leaving it on the floor too. He didn't think he had touched anything else in the room, but just in case he wiped the door handle and the door itself and all the chairs and the refrigerator. Then he wiped everything a second and third time, trying to avoid looking at Amy. When he thought he was done, he noticed blood on his right sleeve. He rinsed it in the sink, ringing out as much of it as he could. He didn't think there was blood anywhere else on him.

There were voices in the hallway. He was certain that people had heard Amy fall and were coming to see if she was all right. But the voices—a man and woman laughing, talking about the storm—passed, and he heard their footsteps, fading gradually as they went upstairs.

David was drenched in sweat. Accidentally seeing Amy's wide-open eyes, he almost gagged. He listened carefully, making sure no one was coming. Then, using the dish towel, he opened the apartment door very slowly and peaked outside to make sure there wasn't anyone in the hallway. The coast seemed clear so he tossed the dish towel on to the kitchen counter and let the door close.

He couldn't remember leaving the apartment building. It seemed like he suddenly appeared, walking in the snow on Morton Street. There didn't seem to be anyone around outside the building who could have seen him leave. He prayed no one had heard the attack, but he didn't know how this could be possible. The only thing he had going for him was that he didn't think Amy had screamed very much, if at all.

The snow was coming down even harder now, reducing visibility. Any footprints he had left would soon be covered.

He walked crosstown, trying to think about the snow so he wouldn't think about anything else. But other thoughts kept creeping in. He didn't know why he had to pick up that frying pan. Now there was no way he could say it had been an accident or self-defense.

At Astor Place, he took the subway uptown. Sitting in the mostly empty subway car, he kept seeing Amy's limp body and the puddle of blood. But now it wasn't the idea that he had killed her that upset him as much as the idea that she might not be dead.

Thirteen

THE SNOW WAS still falling lightly when Billy Balls drove out of the Brooklyn Battery Tunnel. As he approached the toll booth he warned the little girl he had tied up in the back seat to keep her stupid mouth shut.

"I don't want to have to hurt you or nothing," he said, "but I'll do it if you fuck this shit up."

The girl didn't say anything—how could she with that sock stuffed in her mouth? Billy kept hearing her crying quietly, like she'd been doing since he'd picked her up.

"Shut the fuck up, God damn it!" he screamed.

He slapped the top of the dashboard once with his open hand, then turned the radio up. Dion was singing "The Wanderer," and Billy started singing along.

"Now I'm the type of guy, who'll never settle down..."

The black lady working the toll booth seemed so bored with her job that she didn't even look at Billy, no less at the bulge under the blanket on the back seat.

"That a girl!" Billy screamed over his shoulder as he angled his LeSabre on to the Belt Parkway. "Just keep on doing what I say and everything's gonna be all right!"

When "The Wanderer" went off and some pussy Elvis song came on Billy had a feeling that he had forgotten something. He hated that feeling. It happened all the time since the accident. It was like suddenly not being able to recognize his own face in a mirror.

"Fuck! Fuck! Fuck!" he screamed, then he banged his fist against the dashboard. His car swerved on an icy patch, nearly causing a collision with the pickup truck in the right lane. The pickup moved alongside Billy's car and Billy gave the driver the finger. "Fuck you, cock-sucker!"

Billy tried to calm down, taking slow, deep breaths. He'd put the girl in the car, just like Joey had said. Well, not exactly like Joey had said, but what was he supposed to do? The girl didn't want to get in and he didn't want to drive back into Manhattan tomorrow and sit double-parked all day like a dickweed. It was the smart-ass girl's fault anyway, not his. Saying "If my dad was in an accident, my mother would have told me someone was gonna pick me up." Then it hit Billy how stupid the plan was. Why would a little girl believe a guy in a ski mask? And this girl was smart, going to private school and shit. She was like one of those little girls in—what's the name of that movie used to come on Channel Nine?— *Mary Poppins*, except without the faggy British accent.

But it was probably a stupid idea to get out of the car, right in front of the school, then grab the girl and drive away. He'd definitely have to lie to Joey about that part. But at least it worked. He'd done it so fast he was positive no one had seen and if he didn't do it what was he gonna do, drive back to the school tomorrow and offer the girl candy to get into the car? The little brat would probably tell her mommy and daddy about the whole thing and he'd be lucky if the cops weren't there, waiting to take him away.

Driving along snow-covered Ocean Parkway, passing all the apartment buildings where the old Jewish people lived, Billy felt a lot better. That sometimes happened too—one second he'd be sure he'd forgotten something, the next second his mind was back to normal. The only trouble was he never knew whether he was really all right or if he had just forgotten that he had forgotten something.

Billy loved Brooklyn. Although sometimes he got fed up with all the fuckin' niggers in his neighborhood and he'd been thinking about looking for an apartment in Bay Ridge or Sheepshead Bay. But he could never understand guys like Joey who moved to Manhattan. They became fuckin' snobs and it was like they didn't even know it. Joey was always acting like he was above it all, not coming out to Brooklyn for card games anymore or to pick up some action in Coney Island. Just thinking about those black chicks with the fat lips and the big asses was giving Billy a hard-on.

* * *

When Billy arrived in his driveway and shut off the engine and stereo he warned the little girl to stay quiet. Before he picked her up and brought her into the house he wanted to make sure that little nigger next door wasn't spying on him. The snow was starting to come down pretty hard now and he could imagine that kid being outside, building a snowman with his little spook friends.

After waiting outside the car for about a minute, Billy decided enough was enough. He lifted the girl up on to the back seat and said "Watch yourself now so I don't have to hurt you," and then he picked her up. She still had the black masking tape around her head covering her eyes, and another few pieces over her lips, covering the sock stuffed in her mouth. He moved quickly, not bothering to zip up his khaki army-style winter jacket. He carried her into the house through the side door. The girl was still crying. "All right, shut the fuck up," he said, carrying her down the steps into the dark basement. At the bottom of the stairs he flicked on a light. The place was a mess. Paint cans, rusty gardening equipment, a couple of old bicycles and other junk was strewn all over the place. It was as cold and damp as it was outside.

Billy opened an old folding chair, brushed away the dust and cobwebs, and set the girl down.

"You better be a good girl and not give me any problems otherwise you're not gonna have a good time here. Sorry, but I'm gonna have to keep that sock in your mouth and your hands and legs tied, but I'll take the tape off if you want. You want me to take the tape off?"

The little girl nodded.

Billy pulled the tape off the girl's mouth, taking with it a few of the girl's hairs. She made a muffled noise into the sock.

"Shut the fuck up or I'll put the tape right back on."

The little girl's eyes were still covered, but he liked the way her mouth looked. She was definitely a good-looking little chick. She reminded him of the girls he used to neck with in third and fourth grade. Nice smooth face, not packed with zits like the girls he'd been fucking lately. She had a nice mouth—white teeth, like she never smoked a cigarette in her life, and her breath didn't smell like a garlic pizza. She had thin pink lips that looked especially cute the way they were spread around the sock. He wondered if she had a boyfriend. She must be eleven years old and there were a lot of eleven-year-old sluts in the neighborhood when he was growing up. But she didn't seem like the slutty type. She was the nice, goody-two-shoes type of girl who would always be kissing the teacher's ass after class. She was definitely not the type of girl who would have liked him in the seventh grade.

Running the back of his hand gently against the little girl's cheek, Billy said, "Anybody ever tell you you're really cute?"

Now tears were streaming out from under the tape, down the girl's cheeks.

"Why the fuck are you crying? That was a compliment. Wait till you grow up and start putting on weight, losing your looks. You're gonna wish for a nice guy like myself to come along and tell you that you look cute. You got a boyfriend?"

The girl was still crying.

"Answer me. You got a boyfriend?"

Finally, the girl shook her head slowly.

"When I was your age I had tons of girlfriends. I know it's hard to imagine now, being bald and shit, but I was pretty cute back then. I was a real guido, you know what I'm saying? I was like that guy, what's his name, on that TV show? Fuck, I hate when I forget things. Anyway, I was like him, the guy from that show everybody wanted to go out with. I had the black slicked-back hair, a lot of grease in it, and I used to dress really cool. In junior high I had a black leather jacket. I had an earring too—not in the right ear, I wasn't a fuckin' faggot—in the left. It was a little silver lightening bolt and all the chicks were crazy about it. Chachi. That's his name. I forget his name in real life. Something Italian. Hey, stop cryin'!"

Billy put his loose fist under the girl's chin and gently tilted her head up.

"There we go, you don't gotta be afraid of me. What am I gonna do, bite you? I'm just doing this 'cause I owe a friend a favor. We're just gonna get some money from your mommy and daddy and then I'm gonna let you go. Hey, I got an idea. You want me to take the sock outta your mouth? I'll do it, but you gotta promise me you're not gonna scream. If you scream I'm gonna put the sock right back in and I won't ever take it out again. You promise you're not gonna scream?"

The girl nodded. Billy took the sock out of her mouth and the girl coughed. Now Billy had his hand on her thigh.

"What's the matter, you sick or something? I'll tell you what. I got an electric heater here someplace. I'll find it, clean it out, and put it on for you tonight. I'd bring you upstairs with me but—" he almost said Joey's name—"this guy I'm workin' with said I gotta keep you down here at all times in case the police barge in here or something. You know you got nice teeth. Smile and let—" he almost said his own name—"and let me see what they look like."

Billy lifted the girls's upper lip with his thumb.

"Nice. I bet you don't get any cavities."

"I'm thirsty."

"Did I tell you to talk? You listen to me, okay, or I'm gonna get very angry. I'll get you water, I'll get you soda, I'll get you whatever the fuck you want, but I thought first we'd play a little game. You like games? Don't answer. I'll do all the talking from now on."

Billy stuck his thumb in the girl's mouth.

"You like the way that feels, don't you? It feels like a lollypop. So just keep pretending. Pretend my thumb's a nice juicy lollypop."

Billy was starting to feel the way he did when he thought about the black chicks in Coney Island. Then the pain started. It took him a couple of seconds to realize the pain was coming from his right thumb and a couple of more seconds to realize that the girl was biting down on it.

"Damn it!" He screamed, trying to get his thumb loose, but the girl was biting down hard and wouldn't let go. Billy lifted the girl out of the chair by her hair and finally broke free.

"You little cunt!"

He slapped the girl across the face. The pain in his thumb was unbearable and his blood was dripping onto the floor. He stuffed the sock back into the girl's mouth and went upstairs. He ran cold water over the wound, revealing the girl's teeth marks just above his knuckle. It took a while, but he finally got the bleeding to stop. He was mad at himself for hitting the girl. He decided to be nice to her from now on, try to get her to like him.

When he went back downstairs the girl was crying again. Billy said, "Let's talk about dinner. You like Spaghetti-O's?"

Fourteen

WHEN DAVID SAW the police officer sitting on his couch and Leslie in a chair across from them, crying into a ball of napkins, he was certain that Amy was alive and that he was going to spend the rest of his life in jail. He imagined how claustrophobic it would feel, like being stuck in an elevator twenty-four hours a day.

Leslie looked at David and started sobbing even louder. David wondered when the cop was going to handcuff him.

The cop, who had a bushy mustache and who spoke with a heavy Bronx accent, said, "I think I should probably brief you on the situation, Mr. Sussman."

David decided to play it cool, or as cool as possible. He'd wait to hear what the officer said before he gave anything away. And then he'd refuse to say anything without speaking to a lawyer. He kept his right hand in his pocket, hoping that the blood stain wasn't visible on his sleeve.

"Situation?" David said. "What situation?"

"It appears as though your daughter may have been abducted this afternoon."

David felt a wave of relief. It was only after Leslie looked up and David saw her reddened face and the mascara lines under her eyes that he realized exactly what was going on.

"Abducted? What the hell are you talking about?"

The officer, in a calm, even tone, explained that the children at Jessica's school had been let out early today because of the snowstorm, and that when Leslie went to meet Jessica, she wasn't there. As the officer spoke, Leslie continued to cry, sometimes uncontrollably, and David went over and put an arm around her.

"There has to be some reasonable explanation for this," David said. His mind was still mixed up—pulling him in different directions. How could this possibly be happening? "She's probably at a friend's house. Have you called all of her friends?"

"A detective is actively exploring every possible lead and, despite the snowstorm, the police department is doing everything humanly possible to find your daughter. I just thought it would be best to stay with your wife until you returned."

Leslie, for the first time since David had come home, said in an unsteady voice, "Where were you?"

"What do you mean?" David said. "I've been at my office."

"I've been calling you there all day, ever since..." She was fighting back tears. "Where *were* you?"

David recalled how he had been letting his voice mail pick up all afternoon, thinking Amy was calling him.

"I was tied up in meetings," he said. "I wasn't taking calls."

"I already gave your wife a twenty-four hour number where you can call for updates," the officer said. "Of course we'll alert you as soon as we know anything."

"What about that woman I told you about?" Leslie asked.

"The detectives will look into it," the officer said, "but, to be honest, if all you're telling us is her name is Amy, and she's Asian, around twenty-five years old, I'm not sure we'll have a lot to go on. If you knew where she lived or worked, that would be another thing."

"But I'm positive she's somehow involved in this."

"Rest assured, we'll do what we can," the officer said. "But until you get some sort of ransom call, or until your daughter's been missing for twenty-four hours, we can't even be sure she was kidnapped."

"Find her!" Leslie wailed. "I don't care what you have to do—just find my daughter! Find her!"

After the officer was gone and Leslie finally settled down she asked David if he thought they'd ever see Jessica again.

"Don't be morbid," David said. He'd been crying himself and now the tears were flowing faster. "There has to be some reasonable explanation for this."

"Will you stop being so fucking optimistic? She's gone. Somebody's stolen our daughter from us."

"We don't know that."

"Then where is she?"

"At a friend's. Maybe she forgot to tell you—"

"She's not at a friend's. I just hope to God she's alive."

"It's very busy on Seventy-seventh Street, especially at that time of day. I'm sure nobody took her then, and Jessica's smart enough not to go someplace with a stranger."

"I should've been there. It's all my fault."

"It's nobody's fault."

"I was just sitting here, watching a stupid soap opera...and what about that woman? And what about that cassette? Remember how that cassette was delivered the other day? I forgot to tell the police, but do you think that has something to do with this?"

"What could the cassette possibly have to do with it?"

"I have no idea, I'm just wondering, maybe there was some message on the tape, something that was erased or that we couldn't hear. Maybe we should give the tape to the police."

"I think we should do everything possible, but I'm not sure what good that's going to do. My throat's very dry. I have to get something to drink."

David just wanted an excuse to get away from Leslie. Since she'd mentioned Amy's name, he'd had a splitting headache. Staring at a frying pan on the stove, David couldn't breathe.

"David—"

Leslie's voice startled him. The glass he had just taken out of the cabinet dropped out of his hand and shattered onto the floor.

"What's wrong?" Leslie said.

"Nothing," David snapped. "Shit, where the hell is the broom?"

"Never mind," Leslie said.

David went down the hallway, toward the storage closet. His pulse was pounding, his mouth was dry, and his head was still throbbing.

As he swept up the glass, Leslie stood in the kitchen crying.

She said, "What are we going to do?"

"What can we do?" David said. "We'll wait."

"I've called all of her friends, maybe I should call them again. Maybe there's someone I've forgotten to call."

"You didn't forget."

"How do you know? I mean I don't think I did, but there could've been one person—"

"I said you didn't forget."

"What's wrong with you? Why are you yelling at me?"

"Because you don't listen. I say things once and I have to say them again."

"If you're secretly angry at me—if you think I should've picked her up, I wish you'd just go ahead and say it."

"I'm not angry at you," David said. "I mean just because there's a blizzard, why should you think the kids might be getting out of school early?"

"How dare you be sarcastic!"

"I'm not being anything."

"Bastard!" Leslie shouted. "Stay the hell away from me!"

She stormed out of the living room and slammed the bedroom door behind her. After several seconds of silence David started to feel guilty. He knew that it wasn't Leslie's fault—if anyone was to blame it was himself.

David knew that Amy Lee was behind all of this. If she was crazy enough to stalk him and his family, then she was probably crazy enough to kidnap a little girl. Then David had a thought that sent a sharp pain through the middle of his chest—what if Jessica was in Amy's apartment right now? He imagined her tied up in the bedroom, while he was beating the hell out of Amy in the kitchen. Now David was glad he'd killed Amy; the bitch got what she deserved. David imagined himself going back to Amy's apartment, breaking down the door, and rescuing Jessica. But he knew this would probably be a dumb idea. The police would arrest him and Jessica's testimony would send him to prison for life. He just had to pray that he was wrong, that Jessica wasn't in that apartment.

But what if Amy wasn't dead? It didn't seem

possible that she could have survived, but how could he know for sure? David pictured Amy getting up, her face covered with blood, and making it to a phone and calling for an ambulance. But if she *did* survive, David didn't understand why the police hadn't come to arrest him already. Maybe she had amnesia or had lost consciousness again, or—more likely—maybe she didn't tell the police what happened on purpose. Helplessly, David realized that it would be just like Amy to want to prolong his agony for as long as possible.

At the bedroom door, David pleaded for Leslie to let him inside.

"Come on, Lez. This isn't the time to fight. For God's sake!"

After a few more minutes, David gave up. He waited for his breathing to return to normal, then he went back into the kitchen and finished picking up the glass.

* * *

On TV, Clint Eastwood was staring down one of the bad guys. David wished he could be that cool. He tried narrowing his eyes and stiffening his face, but it didn't make him feel any more relaxed.

A guru—who was also an ex-client—had once given David a mantra. Although he hadn't meditated in years, he tried to breathe in and out, focussing his attention inward. It seemed to be working until Eastwood started shooting up all the bad guys in the saloon. The gunshots sounded like firecrackers going off in David's brain and he saw the image of Amy on the kitchen floor again. He muted the sound and tried to catch his breath. Leslie came out of the bedroom with new mascara marks on her cheeks.

"How in the world can you watch TV at a time like this?"

"I was watching the news," David said. "I thought there might be a story about Jessica."

"Was there?"

David shook his head. Leslie sat down on the couch next to him and hugged him tightly. David thought it was beautiful how he didn't have to apologize to Leslie and how she didn't expect him to. They must have had the best marriage in the world. At that moment, he loved Leslie so much he couldn't imagine what had possessed him to get involved with a woman like Amy Lee. He prayed to God that Amy was dead, that Jessica wasn't in the apartment, and that no one had seen him leave the murder scene. Maybe everything would work out—maybe there was a solution to this nightmare he couldn't imagine.

David and Leslie sat on the couch for what seemed like hours, although it was probably only a few minutes, not talking at all. Then Leslie said, "Let's call the police."

"What for? If they knew something, don't you think they would have called us?"

"You never know."

Leslie called the hotline number. After being put on hold for several minutes, she was told that there had been no breaks in the case. Dejectedly, she sat back down next to David. They sat there silently for several more minutes, staring blankly at the muted Clint Eastwood movie, when she suddenly pushed herself away from David, her eyes wide with excitement and she said, "I've got it!"

David felt like he was strapped into an electric chair and the first bolt had been sent through his body. He was dizzy and the muscles around his mouth went numb. Leslie was talking fast and David caught on late to what she was saying.

"...and now it's happening, can't you see? Her prediction is coming true. She said there was going to be tension and trauma in my life and this is it. What could be worse than having your daughter disappear? But what she didn't say is that she was going to be the cause of my problems. But this proves it—she's definitely involved."

David was relieved. At least Leslie hadn't made the connection about the affair, but how long would it be before she did?

"This is probably all just a big coincidence," David said. "Why would some woman become so obsessed with you that she'd kidnap your daughter?"

Still not quite over the new shock, David's voice was wavering. Leslie hugged him again and said, "I'm telling you, she's involved."

Fifteen

OVER SIXTEEN INCHES of snow had fallen in Central Park and Joey didn't give a shit. He was waiting for the real news to come on, to see if there was any report about a kidnapping on the Upper East Side, but all the news stations were covering the snowstorm like it was goddamn Armageddon.

All last night Joey had watched the news on TV too. Every half hour or so he'd called Billy, but he couldn't get a hold of him. For a while there was no answer, then the phone was busy all night. This morning there was no answer again. Joey wanted to kill him. He'd told him at least three times yesterday to call him, no matter what, as soon as he got home. All the time he knew Billy was going to forget. His eyes were wandering off like he was in never-never-land and a few times Joey had to say "Hey, Billy," just to get his attention.

Joey hoped nothing went wrong. Last night, he'd hardly slept. The stitches in his cheek and forehead were bothering him, but he was also ready for the police to barge in at any second. Billy was such an idiot he could have gotten himself arrested. Joey imagined Billy at the police station opening his big mouth about everything.

"It wasn't me, officer, it was this friend of mine, Joey DePino. It was all his idea. You want his address and phone number?" Joey realized he had nobody to blame but himself, putting his life in the hands of a screwed-up wacko like Billy.

On the news a dumb, geeky-looking guy was in the middle of a snow-covered midtown street interviewing people. "What do you think of the snow? What about you, sir? What do you think of the snow?"

"Fucking pricks," Joey said out loud and changed to a different station.

But all the other networks were covering the snowstorm too. Joey wondered if maybe Billy had gotten the girl, but the police just weren't making it public yet. Maybe they were working on the case quietly, trying to follow up leads. Or maybe Billy hadn't kidnapped her after all. Joey hoped this wasn't the case. Carlos wanted his money in four days and if Joey didn't have it he wouldn't let him get away this time with just a few stitches in his face. Again, Joey saw that goddamn INQUIRY sign light up in his brain, thinking how easily this whole mess could have been avoided.

Just thinking about gambling made Joey antsy. He wanted to be back at a racetrack again, eating some greasy food, breathing in cigarette smoke. He missed the feel of a *Racing Form* or a program in his hands, and the excitement he always felt when he walked into a racetrack at the beginning of the night. No matter what had happened the day before, no matter how much money he had lost, there was always a clean slate, a new race to handicap. And next month was the start of the NCAA playoffs. And before he knew it baseball season would start and then the hockey and basketball playoffs. Life just seemed like a boring waste of time when he didn't have any action going.

Maureen came into the living room. She was dressed for work, looking just as done-up as she had been yesterday. She was wearing a short skirt Joey had never seen before and tons of makeup. Thinking that she looked good for a change, Joey said, "Why the hell are you so dressed up?" and she said, "Because I feel like it."

Joey had no idea what was going on inside that woman's head and he wasn't going to waste his time trying to figure it out.

Maureen was checking her makeup in her compact, humming some song to herself.

"Why are you so cheery?"

"It's the snow. It makes everything so festive."

Joey shook his head.

"Shouldn't you call work first. How do you know—maybe your office is closed today."

"I doubt it. If it is, it'll just be nice to take a walk in the snow."

"Do me a favor, leave me twenty bucks."

"What do you need money for?"

"We're talkin' twenty bucks," Joey said. "I need to fuckin' eat, don't I?"

Maureen put a twenty-dollar bill on the table. She snapped her compact shut then put it away inside her pocketbook.

Later, Joey thought how it was weird to see Maureen so happy, dressing up for work. He might have said something to her about it, gotten more curious, but it was nice to have her in a good mood, not on his ass about money or finding a job, and he didn't want to push his luck.

Joey dialed Billy's number again. During the third ring Billy picked up.

"Where the fuck have you been?"

"When?"

"Yesterday, today..."

"I was here."

"No you weren't, I was calling you."

"I swear it."

"Didn't I tell you to call me soon as you got back?"

"Shit," Billy said, "I knew I forgot something."

"You get the girl?"

"Yeah, I got her," Billy said.

"You did?"

Suddenly, Joey felt sick in the stomach.

"Where is she? Nobody saw you, did they?"

"Nah, I don't think so."

"What do you mean, don't think so?"

"Nobody fuckin' saw me."

"Holy shit. And she's okay? You're feeding her? Where is she, your basement?"

"Yeah, but it's freezing cold down there, man. We didn't think about that. It's a good thing I had an electric heater laying around."

"Whatever you do, don't bring her upstairs."

"What do you think, I'm stupid?"

"But everything went good yesterday? She got right in the car?"

"Not exactly."

"What do you mean?"

"She wouldn't *get* in, I had to *get* her in. But she's here now and that's what's important, right?"

"Jesus H., Billy. Nobody saw you. You sure nobody saw you?"

"Positive. Hey, how about a little congratulations here? I do what I'm supposed to do, get the fuckin' kid, and this is the thanks I get?"

"This ain't over yet," Joey said. "Getting the kid was one quarter of what we gotta do. Anyway, we probably shouldn't be talking about this on the phone. We have to meet this afternoon, four o'clock in McDonald's at the Junction, Nostrand Avenue. You writing this down?"

"What?"

"What I just told you."

"Nostrand Avenue."

"What time?"

"Stop quizzin' me."

"Then tell me."

There was silence then Billy said, "Six o'clock."

"No, four. *Four*, you idiot. I gotta spell it for you?"

"Don't call me a fuckin' idiot."

"Write it down."

"I wrote it already."

"This is serious, Billy. We can't fuck this shit up. What I mean is, don't think just because you got the kid this thing is over. I need you to concentrate now with all your might."

"I am."

"And remember, whatever you do, don't mention my name."

There was silence again and Joey knew something was wrong.

"What? You didn't say something stupid, did you?"

"No," Billy said.

"Then what?"

"Nothing."

"I could tell you did something wrong. Tell me."

"I didn't do nothin'. I mean I didn't say your name or nothin'. I just said I'm helpin' out a friend."

"Why the fuck did you say that?"

"I couldn't help it."

"Like the words just flew out all by themselves?"

"It's no big deal. Jesus. It's not like she knows who any of my friends are."

"But what if the cops catch you? What if they talk to the girl? The first thing they're gonna want to do is run a check on all your friends—see if there's any connection. When they get to me they're gonna talk to Maureen and that's it."

"Hey, if the cops catch me don't think I'm not bringin' you into this. It's just like the shit at the paint store—one guy gets caught, everybody gets caught. You think I'm gonna take the fall for you on this shit? Yeah, right. I'm tellin' them it was your idea 'cause it *was* your idea."

"All right," Joey said. He remembered how screwed up Billy was and how he was liable to do anything, no matter how stupid. "Never mind. It's probably not as bad as it seems. Just don't say nothing else, all right?"

"Hey, you think I want to go to jail with you?"

* * *

When David went down to get some coffee he saw the crowd of reporters in the lobby. If he had done nothing they probably would have ignored him. But by stopping and staring at them, he might as well have announced through a bullhorn that his name was David Sussman.

He tried to get back into the elevator, but the doors had already closed. When he turned back around the reporters and microphones and cameras were in his face.

"Excuse me, Mr. Sussman."

"Can we speak to you for a few moments, Mr. Sussman?"

"Would you like to make a plea to your daughter's abductors, Mr. Sussman?"

Then the questions came so furiously he couldn't make them out. The doorman and one of the building's maintenance men tried to keep the reporters back, but there must have been fifteen people firing questions at once. Finally, the elevator doors opened. David fended off the crowd and, after the doors opened and closed several times, he was alone again.

Back in the apartment, Leslie was on the phone in the kitchen. The way she was crying hysterically, David knew she was talking to her mother. He went to the bathroom—he was so nervous he had diarrhea—and then he showered and shaved. Despite everything else on his mind, he couldn't help noticing how old and haggard he looked. The bags under his eyes had darkened and now stretched all the way to his nose and new wrinkles had formed on his forehead.

When he came out of the bathroom, Leslie was still on the phone. David turned on the TV in the living room to Channel Seven and a picture of Jessica was being shown. It was her school picture from last year, a blown up version of the one displayed on the bedroom night table. She was smiling widely—probably saying "cheese" —and the flashbulb had brightened her hazel eyes, making them seem as though there were tiny lights in the center of each of them. David wondered how the media was able to get a hold of the picture so quickly.

Leslie was standing in the living room, her eyes so bloodshot they looked like they were bleeding from the corners. David said, "Did you see the picture of Jessica on TV?"

"It was on before, too. My parents are coming to New York."

"You sure that's a good idea?"

"Why? You don't want them here."

"No, that's not it at all," David said, knowing he wasn't sounding very convincing. He couldn't stand Leslie's parents and Leslie knew it. "It's just that with your dad's heart trouble and the way your mother tends to get hysterical—"

"What was I supposed to tell them? They want to be here and frankly I think they're entitled to it."

"Whatever," David said.

"Where's the coffee?"

"It's a mad house down there, I couldn't get out of the building."

Glancing at the TV—there was a report on now about the snow—Leslie said, "Any news?"

"If there was, don't you think the police would've called us?"

"You never know. These days the family is the last to know."

David wondered whether this could be true. Then he wondered if the police had discovered Amy's body, or Amy alive, and were conducting an investigation without announcing it to the public.

Leslie was saying something else.

"What?" David said.

"Don't you listen to me? I said what are we supposed to do, stay cooped up in the apartment like prisoners?"

"Unless you want to go down there," David snapped back at her.

"I need some coffee or I'm gonna pass out."

"Then why don't you eat something?"

Leslie lighted a cigarette.

"What are you doing?"

"What does it look like I'm doing?"

"It looks like you're trying to kill yourself."

Leslie took a long, aggravated drag.

"It relaxes me."

"You'll relax in your coffin."

Leslie took another drag then put the cigarette out in a ceramic bowl on the coffee table. She sat down next to David and said, "You think we'll ever see her again?"

"Yes."

"How do you know?"

"I just do."

"What if she's gone? I was thinking about this before when I was on the phone with my mother—I should never've had that operation."

"Will you stop it?"

"It's true. I know it's terrible—I mean I want Jessica back more than anything in the world—I'd give my life for her right now. I'm just saying if she didn't—that would be it. We'd never have children *or* grandchildren. We'll just be alone forever."

"I don't want to talk about it."

"But what if the operation can't be undone? What if I'm too old? Lot's of women—"

"I said I don't want to talk about it."

Sixteen

It was probably the most unforgettable day of Maureen DePino's life. In the morning, she was so nervous about her date with Pete that she couldn't concentrate on any of her work at the office. Around ten o'clock, she called Leslie, thinking this would help ground her, but Leslie didn't seem to want to talk. "I just walked in the door," she said and it wasn't like Leslie to get rude like that. Maureen wondered if maybe Joey had said something to David the other night to piss them off.

As she rode down in the elevator to the lobby where she was supposed to meet Pete, Maureen decided that the last few days must have been some kind of dream. After all, nothing good ever happened to Maureen DePino. There was no way a gorgeous, intelligent man like Pete would be interested in a woman like her. There had to be something wrong with him—he was probably an asshole who *seemed* like a nice guy. But, remembering how polite and sweet he was, Maureen couldn't believe this was true. If she wasn't dreaming up the whole thing, maybe it was all part of some practical joke. She must have some enemy she didn't know about who had planted Pete at St. Vincent's Hospital and there was no way in the world he was going to actually show up.

Certain that Pete wouldn't be there, Maureen actually had to catch her breath when she saw him standing by the concierge desk, holding a single red long-stemmed rose. He looked even better than she remembered—if this were possible. He'd been sitting down most of the time in the waiting room, and when he got up to leave Maureen was so self-conscious she hadn't taken a good look at him. He was well over six feet tall and had broad, strong shoulders. He was wearing a brown leather jacket and khaki pants. Although he had some fat on his stomach, unlike Joey, he carried the extra weight well. He had combed his dirty blond hair back away from his tan, weather-beaten face and his eyes were the same bright, sparkling blue she remembered. If she had seen him in the street she would have guessed he was an ex-football player.

"This is for you."

Maureen was still so frazzled it took her several seconds to realize what he had said. She thanked him awkwardly and they walked on to the avenue. The snow was starting to come down heavier now and Pete was saying something about the storm that Maureen was only half paying attention to. All she could think about was how she looked—was her makeup too caked on?—and what she would say if there was a lull in the conversation. Earlier, in the office, she had made a mental list of topics to bring up, but now she couldn't remember any of them.

"Sorry, what was that?"

"I said you look especially beautiful this afternoon."

Maureen blushed. She wasn't used to people complimenting her and she was terrified that Pete would notice how she was blushing and that he would start laughing. But if Pete *had* noticed the redness in Maureen's cheeks he wasn't going to say anything about it because he had already branched off into some other story about something that was happening at his job. A bomb could have exploded in the middle of East Forty-ninth Street and Maureen wouldn't have noticed it. Time was so out of whack that it seemed like a few seconds after Pete had said that she looked especially beautiful today, they were standing in front of the Rockefeller Center ice skating rink. Maureen barely noticed that they had walked over four blocks in the snow to get there.

They went down to the cafe alongside the rink. Although Maureen ordered a sandwich she knew there was no way she'd be able to eat it.

Gradually, she relaxed and started to participate in the conversation without thinking about how she looked or what topics to bring up. Maureen had never felt more comfortable around a man than she did around Pete. She felt like she was having lunch with an old friend. Although they didn't have much in common—Pete was from New Jersey and had a business degree from Rutgers—they had the same sense of humor. A few times, Pete made Maureen laugh so hard she couldn't catch her breath, and she didn't care what she looked like or how she sounded. She couldn't remember the last time she'd laughed or even smiled at anything Joey had said.

Pete was the man Maureen had always dreamed of marrying. Besides being extremely good-looking and having a great personality, he had a confident way about him that Joey definitely didn't have. Although they didn't look at all alike, Pete somehow reminded her of David Sussman. Like David, Pete was the type of man who would always be there for his wife and his family, who would always be confident and strong no matter what happened. From the way it sounded, Pete was a real bread winner too. He talked about the two-family apartment building he owned in Hoboken and the weekends he spent on the Jersey shore. He also talked about having a financial advisor and wanting to retire before he was fifty, so he must have been doing pretty well in the carpet business.

After Pete paid for the meal with a Gold Card, they went back up to the ground level and looked down at the skating rink. The snow was coming down pretty hard now and the gusting wind in Rockefeller Plaza was whipping the flakes around. Only a few skaters were still outside. As Maureen and Pete watched the people skate around the oval, they talked and laughed, or were just quiet, enjoying the wintery scene. Maureen wished the Christmas tree was still up. She always thought it would be so romantic to be with a man she loved under the giant tree. Every winter she asked Joey to come with her and he'd always say, "What am I gonna win looking at a Christmas tree?" and she'd wind up going alone or not at all.

Pete was holding her hand. It seemed so natural to Maureen that she hardly noticed it. Even though they were both wearing gloves, she felt like she could feel the heat of his body seeping through. She looked at her watch and saw it was almost one-thirty. Her boss would kill her for taking such a long lunch. But she didn't want to leave Pete. Suddenly, all she could think about was Joey. She didn't want to spend another night fighting, trying to stop him from gambling. She wanted to be happily married and she wanted her children to have a father like Pete.

"What's wrong?"

Maureen was still looking down at the skaters, watching a man and woman holding hands, skating around the rink together.

"Nothing," Maureen said. "It's just...forget about it."

"I hope you're having a good time," Pete said, "'cause I know I am."

"You kidding me? This is like the best time I've ever had. It's *too* good."

"What's that supposed to mean?"

"It's just...forget it," Maureen said. "I shouldn't've said anything."

Maureen wiggled her hand free of Pete's grip.

"What's wrong?"

"Nothing," Maureen said.

"Come on," Pete said. "Let me guess. You have a boyfriend."

"I wish," Maureen said. "I should've told you the other day in the hospital. There's more than another guy. I wasn't wearing my ring in the hospital but...I didn't want to lie to you. I mean I didn't think a guy like you would ever...I mean it's not like I'm happy or anything. Things are real shitty with us. He's a compulsive gambler and I can't even get him to admit it. All we ever do is fight. I've been thinking about doing something—I don't know if I'd leave him—then you came along. I'm sorry, okay? I just can't believe any of this is happening."

Pete was kissing Maureen. His tongue was a magic wand and he was holding her so tight she was actually starting to get excited. No one had ever kissed Maureen as passionately before. Sometimes Joey went weeks without even giving her a peck on the cheek.

Pete walked Maureen back to her office building. They arranged to meet for drinks the next day after work and then Pete gave her a long goodbye kiss. Maureen couldn't stop thinking about Pete all day. One of the lawyers in the office told her to "stop daydreaming" and get back to work. Usually, something like that would have bothered Maureen, but today her job was her least concern in the world. What did she care if some ugly, sleazy lawyer treated her badly? He was just a miserable man who had nothing going on in his life so he spent his time spreading his misery to others. Life was too short to spend worrying about people like that.

Maureen wished she had someone to talk to about her date. She thought about calling Leslie again, but Leslie wasn't in a very talkative mood when Maureen had called earlier. Come to think of it, Leslie hadn't seemed like her old self in a long time. That night at dinner she seemed much quieter than usual and she didn't look very healthy either. Maureen hadn't seen her so thin since she had anorexia as a teenager. Maureen decided that the next time she got together with Leslie she'd ask her about it, but she'd have to approach it carefully. Leslie was a very private person and she didn't like to talk about her problems.

Usually, Maureen walked home from work, but because of the snowstorm she decided to take the Fifty-seventh Street bus across town. Staring out the window at the driving blizzard, Maureen felt like she was waking up from a dream. Was she crazy, making another date for tomorrow? It didn't matter how nice and how good-looking Pete was, she was a married Catholic woman. Getting a divorce would be a big enough sin, but there was no way she could start dating another man while she was still in wedlock. Although Maureen didn't feel at all guilty for kissing Pete it was still a sin, and she planned to go to church one day this week to confess.

Then she came home and saw Joey sprawled out on the couch in his underwear, his left leg crossed over his right knee, picking at his toenails.

"Did you bring home food?"

"No."

"For Chrissakes."

To hell with Joey DePino, Maureen thought. She'd wasted enough of her life trying to change him and blaming herself and being miserable. Besides, as Leslie had said, how did she know what Joey was doing when he wasn't home? All those nights she'd thought he'd been at the racetrack, there could have been one time Joey had really been with another woman.

In the morning, Maureen was humming the tune of her favorite song—David Cassidy's "I Think I Love You"—as she checked her makeup in her compact when Joey said, "Why are you so cheery?"

"It's the snow. It makes everything so festive."

Joey shook his head, laughing to himself.

New York after a blizzard was the most beautiful city in the world. The snow was still falling lightly and the few cars on the streets were moving slowly and quietly. Of course this wouldn't last forever. The snow would turn brown, then gray, then black, but at least right now Maureen felt as if she were taking a walk through heaven.

This time, when she met Pete in her office building lobby for lunch, he was holding a bouquet of at least a dozen red, pink, and yellow roses. Maureen kissed Pete passionately, unconcerned whether someone from work or someone Joey knew saw them.

The snow had already started to turn into brown, slushy puddles, yet walking, holding hands with Pete, Maureen felt like they were in their own private world.

Not that she really cared, but after about fifteen minutes had passed and they had walked all the way down to Thirty-fourth Street, Maureen asked, "So where's this restaurant we're going to?"

"You'll see."

They walked another few blocks. Normally, Maureen would feel tired and short of breath from doing so much walking, but now she didn't care. At East Twenty-ninth Street, they stopped in front of the Hotel Deauville.

"This isn't a restaurant."

Smiling, looking at her contently with his Paul Newman eyes, Pete said, "I figured we could order in."

Maureen hesitated, but only for a moment; the image of Joey picking his toenails made up her mind.

Pete had reserved a quiet room in the back of the hotel for the afternoon. As soon as he shut the door to their room he pushed Maureen back against the wall. He kissed her hard. One of his hands was in her hair; the other was sliding higher under her dress. He whispered, "Tell me when to stop."

Maureen never said a word.

Seventeen

JESSICA SUSSMAN KNEW what a naked man looked like. Lots of times she'd walked into her parents' bedroom by accident while her dad was undressing and seen his penis—she thought it was such a silly word—which looked to her like a little pink mushroom growing in a patch of brown grass. At school, Jessica and her girlfriends talked about penises and sex all the time. Her friend Rachel's sister Karen, who was in the eighth grade, had already gone all the way with Danny Lipman.

Jessica's arms and legs hurt from being tied up for so long and the tape around her eyes was so tight she couldn't even cry. Her mouth was dry and her throat felt the way it did that time she had tonsillitis. When the man took the sock out of her mouth to feed her, she could hardly talk. She asked the man if he could make the tape on her eyes looser and he said all right, as long as she promised to be a good little girl. When the man loosened the tape she started to cry and cry until the man told her she better stop crying or he'd put the tape back on tight and never make it looser again.

She didn't think she was ever going to be able to fall asleep, but somehow she did. She dreamt it was the biggest snowstorm in the history of New York and the drifts were as high as buildings. When she woke up, the man was next to her again; she hated the way his breath smelled like Spaghetti-O's. She wanted to stay asleep, dreaming, but she couldn't, so she just squeezed her eyes tight and imagined she was in Central Park, playing with her dad in the snow.

Later, the man asked her if she wanted more Spaghetti-O's. She hated Spaghetti-O's and that was all the man kept feeding her—Spaghetti-O's and Pepsi. She ate the food anyway because she was hungry and because she didn't want to starve to death. She knew that eventually the police and her dad would catch this man and punish him, because her mom and dad always promised that they would never let anything really bad happen to her.

* * *

At a quarter to four, Elaine and Alan Schlossberg arrived at the Sussmans' apartment. David had fallen asleep in front of the TV and now woke up to the combined nightmare of everything that had happened during the past twenty-four hours and the grating voice of Leslie's mother in the living room.

When David came into the living room Elaine was hugging Leslie and Alan was sitting on the couch opening his suitcase. Elaine was short and chubby with bleached blonde hair. Alan was a few inches taller than Elaine and he was bald and extremely skinny. David had always thought that Alan was the dullest man he'd ever met and he found it nearly impossible to strike up a conversation with him.

"David, how are you?" Elaine said. She came over

and hugged him, as usual leaving a stain of pink lipstick on his cheek. "This is so terrible. It's like a nightmare."

Alan stood up briefly to shake David's hand, then went back to rummaging through his suitcase, coughing up mucous into a handkerchief.

Leslie told her parents how there had been absolutely no breaks in the case and then, as she started to cry, her mother consoled her.

"Leslie, what happened to you?" Elaine said, squeezing her daughter's upper arms, then her ribs. "You're disappearing."

"I am not," Leslie said.

"Alan, look at her," Elaine said. She waited for Leslie to make eye contact with her. "What do you weigh?"

"My normal weight."

"Your normal weight, sure. Look how she tries to cover it up, Alan, wearing loose clothing, just like when she was sixteen. And look at those dark circles under her eyes. She's anorexic again."

"Are you anorexic again?" Alan asked, not looking up from his newspaper.

"No," Leslie said.

Now Elaine looked at David.

"And what's wrong with you, you don't notice? What would she have to do, turn into a skeleton before you cooked her some food?"

"I think she looks fine," David said.

"Fine!" Elaine said. "What planet have you been living on? You hear that, Alan? She's a sick girl. If she keeps going like this she'll be back in the hospital."

"I'm not a girl."

"What do you mean, you're not a girl? You're my girl."

"I'm a woman and can we please stop talking about this now?"

"Eat something," Elaine said. "I'll cook some food. You want some French toast, *matzo brie*?"

"I'm not in the mood to eat."

"Of course you're not in the mood to eat."

"Dad, will you please tell her—"

"This is all your fault," Elaine said to David. "Maybe if you had sex with your wife once in a while you'd notice what she looked like."

"*Mom.*"

"You know when you took those wedding vows and said 'till death do you part' that meant 'have sex till you part' too."

"Mom, can you stop this? I'll throw you both out of here right now. I can't believe you're acting like this now!"

There was a short, awkward silence, then Elaine put her arm around Leslie, her eyes filling with tears.

"I'm sorry, *pushky*," she said. "I was just so upset about little Jessica I couldn't help thinking about my own little girl. Come on, let me make you something. You have to keep your strength up."

Elaine made French toast. The mood at the dining-room table was somber. Elaine and Leslie were sobbing and there were long silences. Alan, meanwhile, was focussed on his food. David watched him cut his food into even, one-inch cubes, then eat individual mouthfuls. The way he was chewing—intently, his eyes closed—David was certain that he was counting his bites. Sure enough, David took his own count and discovered that Alan would take exactly twenty-six bites before releasing the food down his throat.

After Elaine and Leslie cleared the plates, David and Alan remained at the table. David, distracted by his own concerns, barely listened as his father-in-law droned on and on about the new swimming pool that was being installed in their "compound" at the condominium.

The buzzer rang and David leapt up to answer it. It was the doorman, saying a police detective was on his way up.

"What for?"

"He wants to talk to you."

"What do you think they want?" Leslie said, rushing out of the kitchen, becoming hysterical. "You think this is it? They're coming here to tell us—"

"I have no idea," David snapped, feeling short of breath again. They were coming to arrest him now. He was sure of it.

"Let's just pray God is on little Jessica's side today," Elaine said.

They all went into the hallway to meet the detective as soon as he got off the elevator. It seemed like it was taking forever, then the bell rang and the elevator doors opened. Finally, a young, Hispanic man with a thin mustache came out. He looked like he was thirty-five years old. He was wearing a shirt and tie and a suit jacket under a long blue overcoat. He showed his badge and said his name was Detective Dominguez.

"What's wrong?" Leslie said. "Is my daughter dead or alive?"

"I think we should go inside to talk about this," Dominguez said.

"Tell me now. I have to know."

"Are you Mrs. Sussman?"

"Yes, she's Mrs. Sussman," Elaine said. "Tell us for God's sake."

"And I take it you're David Sussman."

"Yes," David said, trying not to shake. "What's going on?"

"Maybe you'd like to tell me that," Dominguez said, staring right at David. David felt like the detective's eyes were the holes in the barrels of a double-barrel shotgun, aiming right at him. Dominguez said to Leslie, "I'm afraid we don't know anything about your daughter, Mrs. Sussman. Fact, till I got here and saw all the reporters and all the officers from your precinct I didn't even know what was going on with that."

"What do you mean?" Elaine said. "What *are* you talking about?"

"I'm here about a homicide. The dead woman's name is Amy Lee."

Eighteen

"AMY LEE? WHO'S Amy Lee?

"It's her! It's the same woman, isn't it?"

"What woman?"

"Amy Lee. The woman who died."

"But who is she?"

"She's a co-worker of Mr. Sussman's."

"A co-worker? You mean you *worked* with this woman?"

Slowly, all the voices merged into one loud noise in David's head.

Leslie was crying. Her face was contorted into an ugly expression. She wailed, "You knew her, didn't you? That's why she was following me. Or was it worse than that? Were you having an affair with her? Is that what was going on? You son of a bitch! You bastard! You knew all along, didn't you? Didn't you?!"

David knew there was no point in lying now. He nodded slowly.

Leslie ran away screaming into the apartment. David started after her, but Dominguez stuck out an arm to stop him.

"Not so fast, guy. I have some questions I want to ask you."

"About what?"

"For starters, where you were last night between five-fifteen and seven o'clock?"

"What the hell are you talking about?"

"It was a simple question."

"I was at work...I mean on my way home from work."

"You sure about that?"

"Where else would I have been?"

"Maybe you were at Amy Lee's apartment, beating her to death with a frying pan."

"My God!" Elaine said hysterically, "I think he's having a heart attack!"

Alan Schlossberg was leaning against the wall, supporting himself with an outstretched arm. His legs were wobbly and his eyes were glassy. Elaine rushed over to help him, then started yelling about his "heart pills" and how it was "all David's fault."

David and Detective Dominguez helped Alan into the apartment and Elaine searched for his heart medicine in a suitcase. When it was clear that Alan was fine and wasn't going to die, Elaine, sitting next to him on the couch, said, "You see what an idiot you are. I told you not to forget to take your pills and look what you do. I should've left you there to die."

"Maybe you should come back some other time," David said.

"I don't think so," Dominguez said. He was holding a small notepad. "You were the last one seen with Amy Lee."

"Was I?" David said.

"Last night you left your office building with her at a little after five o'clock."

"So? I didn't kill her if that's what you're getting at."

"You didn't seem very surprised when I said she was murdered."

"Do you have any idea what I've been going through the past twenty-four hours? My daughter is missing and I really don't give a shit about anything else."

"Arrest him," Elaine said from the couch. "Take the bastard away."

"How did you get home from work last night?" Dominguez asked.

Now David felt sweat dripping down from his arm pits.

"Why are you talking to me about this anyway?" he said. "I hardly knew her."

"You just admitted you were having an affair with her."

"I mean I didn't know her *well*."

"That's not what I hear," Dominguez said. "I talked to some people at the office—they told me all about the little 'thing' you had going with Ms. Lee. The way I understand it it was going on for quite a while, but lately you two had a falling out. Eric Henrikson said you were very upset about it too. He said you told him you weren't gonna put up with any more of Amy Lee's 'bullshit.' So I'm sorry about your daughter Mr. Sussman, but I probably have enough evidence to arrest you right now. So are you gonna answer my questions here or do you want to do it at the precinct?"

David let out a deep breath then said, "I took the bus home."

"You always take the bus home?"

"Sometimes."

"Why not a cab?"

"Because there was a blizzard. You ever try finding a cab in midtown during a snowstorm?"

"How long did the trip take?"

"I wasn't timing it."

"Approximately."

"I don't know. Forty-five minutes—an hour."

"Why so long?"

"It took some time for the bus to come."

"So according to what you told me before, you left your office at five o'clock in the same elevator with Amy Lee, then she went home and you waited for the bus?"

"I'm not sure about the time I left, but that sounds about right."

"That means you got home by at least six o'clock. Is that correct?"

"No," David said. "I didn't get home till closer to seven."

"Then where were you between six and seven?"

"The bus. I guess it took even longer than I thought. Or—that's right—I went to the supermarket. Or I started to walk toward the supermarket on Lexington, but then I decided it was snowing too hard so I came home."

Dominguez had a cynical expression. He said, "Amy's body was discovered at approximately six forty-five p.m., in case you were wondering. A neighbor heard a woman's scream, and then what she described as "loud clanging noises," at approximately five forty-five, and then she called the police. This would give you... I'm sorry, this would give the *killer* enough time to leave the apartment and get uptown well before seven o'clock even if you, I'm sorry the *killer*, took the subway."

"I'm telling you, I came right home last night."

"You mind if I talk to your wife?"

"Yes, I mind. Who the hell do you think you are, bothering us with this bullshit at a time like this? I didn't do anything and nothing I say is going to help you."

"How about if I take a little look around your apartment?"

"How about if you get the hell out of here?"

"I wouldn't talk to me like that if I were you."

"If you want to arrest me, go ahead," David said. "But I didn't do anything and you obviously don't have any evidence that I did anything or you would've arrested me already. So if you're through wasting my time and disturbing my family at a very difficult time I'd appreciate it if you got the hell out of my apartment."

Dominguez smiled over-pleasantly and put his little notebook back into his jacket pocket.

"You want to play this the hard way, we'll play it the hard way," he said. "But I'll be back—with a warrant—and I'll take you in if I have to. But while I'm gone you might want to think about confessing. It could cut some time off your sentence."

*   *   *

Leslie had locked herself in the bedroom. Elaine was at the door, trying to get her to come out. Alan was on the couch, trying to recover from his near heart attack.

David sat down next to Alan, feeling like he had just run in a marathon. In addition to feeling completely wiped out from crying and getting no sleep, his throat was sore from screaming at Dominguez.

David knew Dominguez wasn't through with him. There would be more questions and these would be harder to answer calmly. If there weren't witnesses already there probably would be soon, including the cab driver who had dropped them off on Morton Street. David didn't think the guy would remember him, but all he would have to do is remember picking up two people and dropping off two people. And then there would be physical evidence too. Dominguez had already figured out that Amy had been hit with a frying pan. That meant there had probably been blood on the pan and now David would have to double- and triple-check to make sure there weren't any blood stains on the clothes and shoes he had worn. But there was no way to check if he had left any hair fibers or fingerprints or other traceable evidence at the scene.

David went into the kitchen. He bent over the sink and splashed cold water against his face. As he was wiping himself off with the dish towel, Elaine came in and said, "She won't come out. If she does anything crazy, like tries to jump out the window, I'm holding you responsible. You'll have killed her like you killed that other woman."

"I didn't kill anybody."

"It's none of my business so I don't really care. But my daughter is my business and I want you to stay away from her from now on."

David heard the bedroom door opening. He dashed down the hallway and stuck his foot inside. He forced his way in and then closed the door and locked it.

"Stay away from me," Leslie said.

"What do you want me to say?" David said. "It only happened a couple of times. It was a big mistake, all right?"

"Did you kill her?"

"Jesus—of course not."

David hoped his upper lip hadn't given him away.

"I can't stand you anymore—I can't stand looking at

your disgusting, cheating face."

Leslie started out of the room, then stopped after David said, "I think she took Jessica."

"You know this for a fact?"

"You saw her. She was unstable, completely psycho. She was harassing the hell out of me all week, trying to get me to leave you."

"But she's dead. How could she have Jessica if she's dead?"

"Maybe she was hiding Jessica in her apartment."

"Shouldn't we tell the police that?"

"I'm sure they already searched there."

"How do you know?"

"All right, I'll tell them, but she could be anywhere. Amy could've been working with somebody—a friend."

"Who?"

"I have no idea."

"Now you tell me this. You knew this yesterday, that that woman might have her, didn't you? Didn't you?!"

"No, I'm—I just thought of it now."

"This was important—time was valuable. We could've—"

"I swear, Lez, I didn't know. Honestly, I didn't."

Leslie started to cry. David tried to hug her, but Leslie pushed him away.

Leslie said, "What about the cassette? You think she sent me that cassette?"

"Probably."

"Why? What does that cassette have to do with anything?"

"She sent it to intimidate me. God knows what that woman was thinking."

"And now she's dead. Why is she dead? Who killed her?"

"Maybe her friend did. They could've had a fight about ransom money or something. The friend killed Amy and took Jessica somewhere else."

The story sounded convincing to David. He decided to use it the next time he was questioned by the police.

"But if this friend is crazy enough to kill Amy, maybe he was crazy enough to kill Jessica."

"You don't know the friend is a he," David said. "Besides, I don't think he would do something like that."

"How do you know? Amy was crazy so her friend could be crazy too. And if Jessica's dead it's all your fault. If you told the police yesterday about Amy, where she lives, we might've found Jessica yesterday. But now it's too late. Now she's probably already dead."

"Come on, Lez, you don't know—"

Leslie started beating against David's chest.

"I don't want to hear it. I don't want to fucking hear it! Find her! Find the friend! Find Jessica! Stay out of my goddamn life!"

Nineteen

JOEY WAS AT McDonald's at the Junction of Nostrand and Flatbush eating his second Big Mac. Billy was already a half an hour late and Joey wondered whether he was going to show up at all.

At the next table, a group of teenagers, probably Midwood High School students, were talking loud and laughing, making a lot of noise. Most of them were black and Joey had a feeling that, for some reason, he was the butt of their joke. He thought about getting up and moving to another table, but he didn't want to make it look like he was scared. So he just concentrated on his Big Mac, thinking that all he needed now was to get mugged by a bunch of punks.

"Am I late?"

Billy was standing next to Joey's table, smiling widely.

"Where the fuck have you been?"

"I had to make sure the kid was tied up real good before I left. You didn't want her getting away or getting to a phone, did you?"

"Sit down," Joey said, "we have a lot to take care of."

"You sure you want to sit here?" Billy said. "Why don't we sit in the back, away from the Jungle Bunnies?"

Billy had spoken too loud. Joey was positive one of the teenagers, the big one with dreadlocks, had overheard him.

"You want to get us both killed?" Joey whispered.

"What?"

"This isn't Canarsie or Howard Beach," Joey said. "They're not scared of us here."

Billy made a face, as if Joey was the crazy one, and sat down. "I don't know about you, DePino," Billy said. "Living in the city has made a real pussy out of you."

Billy smiled again through his beard, looking even more demented.

"What are you so happy about?"

"It's a beautiful day," Billy said, "the snow and all that shit. It reminds me of when I was a kid. Remember when we used to build those forts on Albany Avenue and attack the kids from Forty-second Street with ice balls, splitting their fuckin' heads open? Those were the days, man."

"You ready to make the call?" Joey asked, getting aggravated.

Billy was zoning out, looking toward the teenagers.

"Damn it, Billy, we don't have time for this shit."

"I'm here, I'm here."

"We have to rehearse," Joey said. "If you say the wrong thing or don't sound serious enough you'll fuck the whole thing up."

"I call up, I ask for the money."

"It's not so simple. You have to say—you paying attention?—you have to say, 'If you wanna see your daughter alive bring thirty thousand bucks—'"

"That's it? I thought we were gonna ask for fifty?"

"I thought it over—fifty's too much. I don't think he can come up with that much money so fast. So—are you listening?—you say, 'If you wanna see your daughter alive bring thirty thousand bucks in small, unmarked bills, to the Kings Plaza parking lot in Brooklyn, top level, south-east corner, at eight o'clock tomorrow night.' Then say 'If the money's marked or any cops show up I'm gonna shoot the girl in the head.' That's it, that's all you say, then you hang up. Can you remember that?"

"Fuck yeah."

"I wrote it down for you just in case. Read it, memorize it, then say it back to me ten times. And whatever you do, don't, *do not*, let them interrupt you. Just keep reading, then hang up."

"I just thought of something," Billy said. "What if, like in the movies, the cops are tapping into the phone line?"

"So? They come to a phone booth in Brooklyn. Besides, in the movies it usually takes like twenty seconds till they can trace it. By then you'll hang up."

"But maybe the movies are bullshit," Billy said. "Maybe in real life the police can trace the calls right away."

"Just concentrate on what you gotta do," Joey said. "We don't want any complications. I want that girl back to them in two days, tops."

Billy had that psychotic, too-much-teeth grin again.

"Why're you smiling?"

"I ain't smiling."

"How's the girl?"

"The girl? Oh, she's fine."

"You better be taking care of her," Joey said. "You

feeding her? Keeping her warm?"

"I give her a lot of Spaghetti-O's," Billy said.

"Good," Joey said, "because the last thing we want is something to happen to her. Remember, this is my wife's best friend's daughter. She has to stay healthy."

"I'm keeping her healthy all right," Billy said smiling again. Joey remembered what Billy had said in the car yesterday, how he thought Jessica had a cute ass. Then he saw the image of him on top of that retarded girl—his white butt thrusting into her.

"You better not be touching her," Joey said.

"Touching her?" Billy said. "What are you talking about?"

"I don't think even *you're* crazy enough to do a thing like that, but you better not even think about it. I swear to God, if I find out anything happened to that kid I'll come to your house and cut your fucking balls off."

"That's good," Billy said. "You should try out for the movies."

"I'm serious."

"I'm serious too. You're better than Al-fuckin'-Pacino. You're really scaring the shit out of me."

"I wanna get back to the city before Maureen gets home. You gonna read the script to me or what?"

"I was thinkin'," Billy said, "when I meet this girl's father up at Kings Plaza, I should probably have some sort of piece on me."

"Piece?"

"You know, a piece, a rod—a gun."

"No, you shouldn't," Joey said.

"Why not? I mean what if he turns wise guy with me, says he won't give me the money? It's possible he won't give me the money, you know. I need something to make him know I'm serious."

"Where are you gonna get a gun?"

"I got my old man's Colt .45 in my closet. I got the bullets for it and everything."

"No bullets," Joey said. "The gun'll be good enough. Now can we please rehearse?"

Billy had that crazed smile again.

"Tell me it again."

"Tell you what?"

"You know, that Al Pacino shit. How you're gonna cut my fuckin' balls off."

* * *

Leslie and her parents were sitting at the dining-room table, crying into sheets of paper towel, waiting for some news from the police. David was taking a shower. When the phone rang Leslie sprung up to answer it.

"Hello?"

"Mrs. Sussman?"

The harsh, male voice on the other end had a heavy New York accent. Leslie assumed it was a police officer.

"Yes," she said, bracing herself for any news he had. Elaine and Alan were standing next to her, trying to listen.

"If you wanna see your daughter alive bring thirty thousand bucks in unmarked bills to the Kings Plaza parking lot in Brooklyn, top level—"

"Who is this?"

"Never mind. Just listen to me."

"Tell me who this is."

"What is he saying?" Elaine said.

"Hey, who's there with you?" the voice said. "You better not have no fuckin' cops there."

"I want to know who this is," Leslie said.

"I said that's not important, just listen to me." Sounding like a third-grader reading from a piece of paper, he continued, "If you wanna see your daughter alive bring thirty thousand bucks in small, unmarked bills to the Kings Plaza parking lot in Brooklyn, top level—"

"Where is that?"

"What?"

"You said the Kings Plaza parking lot. What is that?"

"It's a shopping center—shut up."

"What?"

"I wasn't talking to you."

"How am I supposed to know where a shopping center in Brooklyn is?"

"It's on Flatbush Avenue, off the Belt Parkway."

David came out of the bathroom wrapped in a towel. He said, "Who's she talking to?"

Elaine and Alan motioned with their hands for David to shut up.

The voice said, "Hey, how many people you got in your apartment?"

"Just my family. I want to know how my daughter is. Is she all right?"

"There better not be no fuckin' cops there."

"There're no police. Where's my daughter?"

"She's fine."

"I want to talk to her."

"She's not here."

"Where is she?"

"Will you just let me finish? Shit, I forgot my place. Oh, yeah, bring the thirty thousand bucks in small, unmarked bills to the Kings Plaza parking lot in Brooklyn, top level—"

"Where am I supposed to get thirty thousand dollars in cash?"

"Who is this?" It was David's voice. He had picked up the phone in the bedroom.

"Who's this?" the voice said.

"This is David Sussman, who *is* this?"

"This is Don't You Worry Who The Fuck This Is, that's who. Now, let me fuckin' finish what I was saying. Thirty thousand bucks in small, unmarked bills, to the Kings Plaza parking lot in Brooklyn, top level, south-east corner, at eight o'clock tomorrow night. If the money's marked or the cops show up I'm gonna shoot the girl in the head."

"I know who you are," David said.

There was silence on the other end—the man hadn't hung up.

"Bullshit," he finally said.

"No, I've seen you," David said. "I know who you are. And if you don't return my daughter right now I'm gonna tell the police—"

"Bullshit," the voice said. "Bullshit. Bull-fuckin'-shit."

"You better not hurt my daughter."

There was a click.

"Hello?" David said.

"Hello!" Leslie screamed.

Leslie had been crying so hard, for so long, that everything was blurred. It was as if someone had hit her very hard, knocking her senseless. David was saying, "...that would be way too risky. We don't know what this guy's capable of."

"But the police know how to handle these things," Elaine said. "They're professionals."

"No police," David said. "This is my daughter we're talking about."

"She's my granddaughter."

"Do you want to go to her funeral?"

"Stop it!" Leslie screamed, putting her hands over her ears, "Just stop it! You're all driving me crazy!"

David waited a few seconds then said, "She's right. Let's not suddenly panic."

"I'd just like to know who this guy is," Alan said.

"He's a maniac," Elaine said. "That's who he is."

"He's probably a friend of Amy's," David said.

"Amy?" Elaine said.

"The woman who was killed," Alan said.

"Why would a friend of that woman's kidnap little Jessica?"

"It's a long story," David said, looking at Leslie. "One we'd rather not get into right now. What's important is that we get him the money and get Jessica home safely."

"There's more than one other guy involved," Leslie said.

"How do you know?" David said.

"He was talking to someone else when I was on the phone with him. He said 'Shut up,' but not to me—there was someone else there with him."

"If there is a third person that makes it even more dangerous," David said. "The other guy might be holding Jessica, waiting to see if the police show up."

"I say we pay the money," Leslie said, "get this nightmare over with."

"I have twelve thousand in a Citibank account," David said.

"Since when?"

"I was saving it for a rainy day."

"Where do we get the rest of the money?"

"Sell some stock."

"Can we do it that fast?"

"We'll have to do the best we can."

"I still think we should tell the police about all of this," Elaine said.

"No police," David said. "I want to handle this alone."

Twenty

WHEN LESLIE TOLD Maureen that Jessica had been kidnapped, Maureen decided it was the wrath of God. Leslie had told her to meet another guy and, because Maureen had done even worse, God was making Leslie pay.

And when Leslie told her about all the other horrible things that were going on her life, this only convinced Maureen even more. She decided that despite what a great guy Pete was and how good he was in bed—she came three times in one afternoon; more than she had in her whole marriage with Joey—she wouldn't see him again. Joey was still her husband and if she kept cheating on him then God would make them all pay.

After she hung up, Maureen went into the living room to tell Joey. Joey was sitting on the edge of the couch, watching a basketball game.

"I just got the most terrible news," Maureen said. She had started to cry.

"Come on, Ewing, you piece of shit!"

"Did you hear what I just said? That was Leslie—Jessica was kidnapped."

Joey was still staring at the television, but Maureen knew he was listening.

"Yeah?" he said.

"Are you listening to me?"

"I'm watching a game here."

"I said Jessica was kidnapped. Their *daughter* Jessica."

"What do you mean, *kidnapped*?"

"That's all she told me. It happened in front of her school."

"Did they find her?"

"Not yet. She was very upset. She didn't tell me much."

"Jesus," Joey said.

"The police are there—she said it's been on the news. I just can't believe it."

"I'm sure they'll find her," Joey said.

"How do you know?"

"Because the police are good at finding kids," Joey said, looking at the TV. "You know how it is. They always *say* the kids are missing then they wind up finding them."

"I hope you're right," Maureen said. "I feel so bad for Leslie. She's been through such a hard time lately. That's the other thing she told me—she found out some awful news about David. He's been cheating on her."

"I already knew about that," Joey said.

"Since when?"

"David told me the other night."

"Why didn't you tell me?"

"Because I thought you'd blab about it to Leslie."

"It's awful, isn't it?" Maureen said. "I've always thought David was such a loyal husband. But that's not all—wait till you hear this—the woman was killed."

Now Joey looked away from the TV.

"What do you mean, *killed*?"

"That's what she said—someone broke into her apartment or something and killed her. The police have been questioning David and everything. Can you imagine the nightmare of that—the same day you find out your daughter was kidnapped?"

"And I thought I had shitty luck."

"So what exactly did David tell you the other night?"

"Just that he was screwing around with some Chinese broad in his office."

"And what did you say?"

"I told him it was wrong to cheat like that. I told him he should think about his wife and kid at home."

Maureen stared at the floor.

"Shoot it! Shoot it!" Joey yelled.

"Joey."

"What?"

"I have to tell you something."

"It's the fourth quarter here."

"It's important."

"Can't it wait?"

"I want you to know that you're important to me— that even though we've been fighting a lot lately and everything I'm...I still love you."

Joey looked at Maureen.

"You feeling all right?"

"Do you love me too?"

"Will you please stop acting like this, getting all worked up just 'cause shit happened to Leslie and David."

"We should go over there tomorrow morning."

"What the hell for?"

"To be with them."

"Come on, Starks! I don't think that's such a good idea."

"Why not?"

"Because."

"Because why?"

"Because we're not family."

"Leslie's my family, or the closest thing I've ever had to one. I have to go over there and I need you to come with me."

Joey yawned, staring at the TV.

"Whatever," he said.

* * *

Joey knew he couldn't say no to Maureen. It would've seemed too suspicious, putting up a big stink, and he didn't want to give Maureen any ideas. She was still in a weird mood, acting all extra-nice and shit about everything. Joey still thought it probably had to do with her feeling sorry for Leslie, but the way her moods had been going up and down lately he wondered if it was something else. After this was all over—after he had his share of the ransom and he paid off Carlos and Frank and everybody else—he was going to put some money aside for Maureen to go see a shrink. Maybe there were some pills or something she could take.

Outside the Sussmans' building, Joey was surprised at the number of TV cameras and reporters. He couldn't believe they were all here just because of the kidnapping. It had to be because of that Chinese woman too.

Walking into the Sussmans' apartment was like walking into a funeral parlor. Leslie's parents were in from Florida—Maureen hadn't mentioned anything about this—and they were sitting with Leslie on the couch crying, holding hands. Maureen was sitting there with them, mopping up her tears, like it was *her* fuckin' daughter that was missing. After Joey said all the "I'm so sorry about your little girl bullshit" he went to sit on a chair in the corner. He was wondering where David was when Maureen asked Leslie the same question.

In a quiet voice, almost whispering, Leslie said, "He went to the bank to get the ransom money."

"Ransom money?" Maureen said. "You didn't tell me anything about ransom money."

Leslie told the whole story about the ransom call, which didn't interest Joey until she said they were planning to do "what the guy told them" and not call the police. Well, there was one thing to feel good about, Joey thought. Maybe this whole mess would have a happy ending after all.

A few minutes later, David arrived. He looked tired and unshaven and had dark bags under his eyes, as if he had just been in a twelve-round fight. He looked ten years older than the last time Joey had seen him, but Joey was most interested in the briefcase he was holding. He assumed he had gone to the bank and taken out at least some of the money.

Maureen repeated her same bullshit to David that Joey could have lip-synched, saying how "sorry" she was, and how "terrible this must be" for him. Then David came and sat down next to Joey and Joey knew it was going to be just like the other night.

"It's crazy, man," David said. "I woke up this morning and the first thing I said to myself was, 'I can't believe this shit is happening to me.'"

There he goes again, Joey thought, saying "shit" and "man" like he was trying to speak a different language.

"Want some advice?" Joey said. "Just do what you gotta do. Bring him the money then leave as fast as possible."

"I'll tell you one thing," David said. "If I ever find out who these motherfuckers are, I swear to God I'm gonna hunt them down and kill them. I don't know how, but I swear I'll do it."

There was suddenly something about David that reminded Joey of Billy. Maureen had told Joey how the police thought that Chinese woman had been killed by someone hitting her over the head with a frying pan. Now Joey imagined David in that woman's apartment, beating her like a maniac. For some reason, it wasn't too hard to picture.

"You sound like what's his name," Joey said, "Charles Bronson."

"Clint Eastwood," David said seriously. "Maybe you'd understand if you had a daughter. There's nothing worse that could happen to a man."

"Don't try to be a hero," Joey said. "Just do whatever the guy tells you to do."

"We think there're two guys."

"Why?"

"When the guy called yesterday Leslie thought there was someone with him."

"Whatever," Joey said. "I'm sure these guys don't wanna get violent. They probably just wanna get their money and get out of there."

Everyone else in the apartment had stopped their conversations and were listening to Joey and David.

"I have an idea," Maureen said to Joey. "Maybe you should go with David tonight."

"I think that's a wonderful idea," Leslie's mother said.

"No, no, I don't think so," Joey said, trying to ignore the sudden sharp pain in his stomach.

"He's right," David said. "The son of a bitch might panic and think Joey's a cop."

"I'm scared," Leslie said.

"I can handle it," David said. "I'll tell you one thing though—I'm gonna take a good, long look at this guy, and when this whole thing's over, some day, not right away—I'm gonna track this guy down. And then I'm gonna track his friend down and I don't know what I'm gonna do, but I'm gonna make them both pay for the pain they've put us through."

As the conversation drifted back to Jessica, Joey started worrying about a lot of things, but mostly worrying about Billy. The guy couldn't even do the phone call right, how was he gonna collect a ransom? Joey was tempted to call the whole thing off, but he couldn't. He only had two more days till Carlos' deadline. Now the stitches in Joey's face were killing him as he remembered what it felt like to be lying on a sidewalk at night, having a box-cutter up to his face and four hard feet taking turns using his head as a soccer ball. This whole thing was already out of control and he had a sick feeling it was only going to get worse.

*   *   *

Billy DiStefano, wearing his ski mask, sat in his freezing cold LeSabre in the corner of the top level of the Kings Plaza parking lot massaging the big bulge in his jeans. He never understood how some guys had trouble getting hard-ons. Even now, in the fifteen or whatever degrees it was, his prick was like a steel bar.

It was getting so annoying he undid his belt and unzipped his Calvin's and started stroking himself. It didn't take very long to come. He wiped his hands on his sweatshirt, feeling at peace again.

He wanted to know where the hell David Sussman

was. According to the clock on his dashboard it was eight o'clock, and wasn't that the time he was supposed to meet him or was it eight-thirty? Shit, he wasn't sure now and Joey had made him throw away that goddamn paper. Joey had yelled at him when he got off the phone outside McDonald's, telling him how he'd done "too much talking." Billy was getting sick of Joey. He was such a city boy now and why wouldn't he just admit it? And he hated the way he always told him things again and again—don't do this, don't do that, don't talk so loud in front of the Jungle Bunnies—like there was something wrong with him. Billy knew there was nothing wrong with him. Yeah, the accident had knocked him around a little, but it was nothing worse than what happens to a quarterback every Sunday afternoon and you don't see anybody treating quarterbacks like they're retards now do you?

Sometimes Billy thought everybody else in the world was nuts.

A car drove up the ramp. It slowed down near Billy's LeSabre, then kept going toward the other end of the parking lot. Billy hoped Joey was right and the guy wasn't going to call the cops. He didn't see why Joey was so sure about everything, like he was a professional criminal or something, and he was glad he'd made it very clear to him how his ass was on the line with this too. Actually, he was surprised Joey didn't pussy out when he told him that, like the time he wouldn't fuck Whatever The Hell Her Name Was with the other guys from the paint store. It wasn't like Joey to actually go through with something like this and Billy knew this gambling shit must be even worse than he made it out to be. He must be in for his lungs, down ten or twenty Gs. He was such a fucking degenerate, since the second grade going to the racetrack every Saturday and Sunday with his old man. Then when his old man dropped dead, somewhere around high school, Joey started cutting class, going to the track, and then at nights he'd hang out at the OTB on Kings Highway with all the scum. He was sixteen years old and he was already like an old man.

Now Billy was really getting worked up, thinking about Joey. He was always so high-on-his-horse, saying shit like "You better not lay a hand on that girl," meanwhile *he* was the fucked up degenerate. There was nothing wrong with getting laid, having a little fun. Women were meant to be fucked, it was as simple as that. It didn't matter how old they were, as long as they had pussies. Like last year he'd met this Irish chick on the street. She said she was eleven years old, but Billy knew she was younger because she didn't even have a bush yet. Now a lot of people would think a chick like that is too young to fuck, but this chick was a dynamo— one of the best lays Billy had ever had. So it just goes to show you—there are no set rules about anything—and Billy didn't give a fuck what anybody said.

Billy saw headlights coming toward him. Whoever it was, the son of bitch wouldn't turn his brights off. Billy shielded his face with his hands, his eyes starting to sting. Then the lights turned off and it took a couple of seconds to refocus. He saw a black or dark blue Mercedes, recent model, must've cost forty grand. Then this tall geek got out. Joey'd said the girl's father was a nerd, but Billy wasn't expecting the guy to be *such* a faggot. Come on, the guy was wearing a shirt and tie under his long, black coat. He remembered the guy's cigarette-smoking wife with the blonde hair and nice shape, walking with the little girl down the street the other day. He knew that a broad like that was only with a geek like this for one reason—money. It didn't have anything to do with the size of his dick or the way he stuck it to her.

The geek was holding a brown briefcase. He stopped in a slush puddle about ten yards in front of Billy's LeSabre. Billy took his old man's Colt .45 out of the glove compartment and tucked it into his *Calvin*'s.

*   *   *

David kept his brights on for a few seconds, trying to see if Jessica was in the car. But all he saw was the one guy wearing a dark ski mask.

He shut off his brights, picked up the briefcase full of money from the back seat, and got out of the car. There was a brisk, frigid breeze against David's back. The gusts were so strong, he felt like someone was pushing him along. There were huge piles of snow at the rim of the parking lot, behind the man's car, and the ground was slick with ice. When David stopped he saw the man in the car reach to his right, then he opened the driver-side door and got out.

"Where's my daughter?" David demanded.

He felt like he was in a movie—Clint Eastwood ready to blow the guy away. The only problems were he didn't have a gun and he wasn't Clint Eastwood.

"First things first," the man in the ski mask said. "Give me the fuckin' money, I'll drop your daughter at the subway tonight."

David recognized the man's voice. It was the same guy who had called him last night. He spoke with a heavy Brooklyn accent, "first" sounding like "fust."

"You're not getting any money till I see my daughter," David said, still being Eastwood. "Now where the hell is she?"

"Yo, yo, hold up a second," the man said. "I'm the one making the rules here, not you. Now don't be a dumb fuck. Just drop the briefcase on the ground and get the hell out of here."

"Is she in the car? Jessica!"

"You fuckin' crazy, nigger?" the man said. "You yell like that again you're never gonna see your daughter alive."

"Listen, cocksucker," David said.

"What did you call me?"

"I'm giving you three seconds to tell me where my daughter is."

"Or what? You turn into a pumpkin?" The man laughed for a couple of seconds, then suddenly stopped laughing and took out a gun. "Drop the briefcase now or I'm gonna fuckin' kill you."

David was trembling. Suddenly, he realized that he wasn't Clint Eastwood—not even close—and he didn't want to die out here in a parking lot. Instinct told him to drop the briefcase, do whatever the man said, but then he thought about Jessica. This guy sounded psychotic and he would definitely kill Jessica instead of turning her loose.

In the next instant, David was sprinting back toward his car. He lost his balance, slipping on the ice, and fell hard on to the ground. At the same moment, he heard three loud noises in rapid succession and then he felt an incredibly sharp pain in his left hip, and then equally sharp pains in his lower back. He realized he had been shot. He remembered the briefcase, and tried to reach back, but the man snatched it just before he could get to it. He struggled to his feet and got back into his car. He didn't remember turning on the engine. The man was already in his car, starting to drive away. David accelerated straight toward him, smashing into the other car almost head on. He saw the man's car spin put of control and crash into a pile of snow. A horn was blaring. Everything went white.

Twenty-One

WHEN LESLIE ARRIVED at the Intensive Care Unit at Kings County Hospital Detective Dominguez said to her, "We need to talk."

"Not now," Leslie said. "I have to see my husband first."

"All right," he said, "but you better not leave here out of any back exits."

As soon as she got word of the accident, Leslie had rushed to the hospital by taxi. She didn't know anything except what they had told her over the phone—that David had been shot and that he was in critical-but-stable condition.

A nurse was still working on David's wounds, but she said that David was awake and alert. Rather than going back out into the waiting room—she didn't feel like talking to the detective right away—Leslie sat on a chair in the corner. A few minutes later, a tall, male doctor with gray slicked-back hair came in and asked Leslie if she was David's wife. Then he said, "Your husband's a very lucky man. One bullet came within a couple of inches of his spinal cord. The second bullet hit his hip and he'll probably need hip-replacement surgery. The third bullet got one of his kidneys. Unfortunately, he went into acute renal failure and we had to remove it, but the good news is that the other kidney's functioning well. He'll be on dialysis for a couple of weeks, but he'll be all right."

Leslie nodded her head slowly and squeezed out a few tears. The doctor excused himself.

The only reason Leslie had rushed to Brooklyn was to find out if David knew anything about where the kidnappers were keeping Jessica. She didn't want David to die, but she was glad to find out that he was in serious pain. He deserved to suffer for the hell he'd put her through. It had occurred to Leslie that Amy probably wasn't the first woman David had had an affair with during their marriage. She felt like an idiot—suffering all these years, taking all of their problems out on herself. The only good thing that had come out of their marriage was Jessica, and now Leslie was afraid she was going to lose her too.

Finally, the nurse told Leslie that she could talk to David, but that he was tired and not to keep him awake for too long. Leslie was glad to see that David had thick, white bandages around his stomach and waist. His eyes were closed and tubes were attached to his body.

David's eyes opened slowly.

"Hey," he said. His voice was cranky, as if he had just woken up.

"Should I go away?"

"No," he said. He reached for her hand. Leslie hesitated—tempted to pull out all his tubes and watch him die in pain—then she held his hand loosely. David smiled.

"Now I feel like new."

"What about Jessica?" Leslie asked. "Did you see her?"

"No," David said weakly. "I thought he was going to kill her so I tried to get away. I think he took the money."

"Should I tell the police?"

"I guess so," David said. His voice was getting weaker. "I didn't get his damn license plate number. At least I don't remember getting it. I guess it's the same thing, huh?"

"There was only one guy there?"

David nodded.

"What about his car?"

"It was blue. I think I might've dented it."

Leslie assumed that the police had taken their Mercedes as evidence.

"It probably doesn't matter," Leslie said. "He probably ditched it by now anyway."

"I need," David said slowly, "I need to tell you something."

Leslie knew an apology was coming and she didn't want to hear it.

"It's not important now," she said.

"I have to," David said, squeezing Leslie's hand tighter. "About everything that's happened. It's important for me to know... I mean if there was anything I could do now...You know how I feel..."

"Rest," Leslie said. "My parents are still here— they'll take care of me."

"I love you."

Leslie didn't answer. She freed her hand, kissed David lightly on the forehead, then left the room without looking back. She was angry at herself for giving in. She didn't love David. Looking at him in the hospital bed, she couldn't help thinking of Amy Lee, that little bitch, squatting on top of him backwards, faking orgasm like some cheap hooker.

Part of her still wanted to go back in there and pull out all of David's tubes. He was a liar. She could see it, even in the hospital bed. She couldn't believe she had wasted eighteen years of her life with him.

A hand tapped Leslie on the shoulder. Dominguez said, "How about we get a cup of coffee now?"

* * *

"Look at it this way," Joey said. "We got the money— some of it anyway—and now we have to give the girl back. That's all there is to it."

Joey was sitting with Billy in the Chinese take-out near the OTB on East Sixteenth Street in Brooklyn. When he'd heard on TV that David Sussman had been shot, Joey thought that was it—he was going to spend the rest of his life in a twelve-by-twelve cell. He'd never be able to bet on anything again, unless he was wagering with packs of cigarettes. But then things seemed to get better. Maureen called Leslie and found out that David probably wasn't going to die and then Joey called Billy and found out that he had gotten most of the money. So Billy had fucked up a little bit by shooting David, but— assuming the cops didn't catch on—at least Joey would be able to pay off most of his debts. If everything went well he might be able to get action in on the NCAAs after all.

Now all Joey wanted was for Billy to stop holding out for more money so he could go into the OTB and play the last race at Aqueduct. He liked the one horse and he knew that if he didn't place the bet it would win easy.

But Billy was still shaking his head. He had a cut on his forehead and a fat upper lip.

"That faggot almost totalled my car and he was

eighteen Gs short on our money. No way, man, no fuckin'
way, I want the eighteen Gs, *plus* another ten Gs, *plus*
damages for my car or I don't care—I'll keep that kid
forever."

"Don't be an idiot," Joey said. "I know it's hard for
you, but try. We got lucky. He could've seen your plates
and the police could've arrested you by now, but they
didn't. Hey—you listening to me?—we can't do nothing
stupid. Let the kid go. Put her out on the Belt Parkway
or something—somebody'll pick her up. We got six
grand a piece, which is twelve grand more than we had
two days ago."

"You know how much it's gonna cost me to fix my
car?" Billy said. "I'm askin' you, you know how much
it's gonna cost me? The front end's tattooed, and even if
I *did* get it fixed, I wouldn't be able to drive it again 'less
I got different plates. I'll probably have to buy a new
car—even used'll cost me a few grand. Then what do I
have left, a thousand bucks? And for what? Puttin' my
ass on the line, shootin' a guy just so you could pay off
your fuckin' debts. Sorry, but you can just go fuck
yourself if you think that."

"Then what do you wanna do?" Joey said
impatiently. The clock behind Billy read 3:55. The horses
were probably already on the track for the eighth race.

"Call her up," Billy said, "the faggot's wife, I mean.
Tell her we want twenty grand."

"We?"

"I—whatever. Plus five grand for my car."

"What if she says no?"

"Then—I don't fuckin' know. All I know is I want
my money and my car. I had a car since I was sixteen.
There's no fuckin' way I'm goin' back to ridin' buses.
What am I, an old lady?"

Looking Billy right in the eye, Joey said, "I'm gonna tell you this straight—there's something fucked up in your head, ever since that car accident. You don't think straight. You can't see it because you're inside yourself—but take it from me—I know what I'm saying. The thing to do right now is forget all about this—just give the girl back and pretend like nothing happened."

"I got a better idea," Billy said. "How 'bout you just give me back your six grand and I use it for a new car?"

Billy had already given Joey his share of the money, and Joey had it inside his blue knapsack. Five grand would go to Frank and Carlos. The other thousand would go toward bills, rent and a couple of nights at the Meadowlands.

"You know I can't do that," Joey said.

"So let me get this straight then," Billy said. "Because you're a degenerate gambler I'm the fuckin' crazy one and I should ride the buses the rest of my life like some nigger?"

"I never said that. And keep it down, will ya?"

"What?" Billy said, loud enough so that the Chinese counter man looked over. "I said nigger not chink. Anyway, the way I see it, I took all the risk so far. I was in that car the other night, in the freezin' cold, puttin' my life on the line. That guy hit me head-on—I coulda gone right through the fuckin' windshield. And if the cops were there, who's the one with the kid in his basement? Who's the one that's gonna be identified? So for now, how 'bout this? How 'bout I call the shots? This is a personal thing now—somebody hurts my car, they're hurtin' me. Now you in with me or not?"

"I'll call the police myself," Joey said. "I'll tell them where the kid is."

"Bullshit!" Billy said, banging his fist against the
table. "You don't wanna go to jail neither and I'll tell the
cops this was all your idea. So what do you say,
Kimosabee?"

"Don't be an idiot," Joey said.

"Look who's talking," Billy said.

Billy left the restaurant. Joey started to get up to go
after him, but quickly realized it would be no use.
Instead he went next door, to the OTB, just in time to see
the one crossing the finish line in front.

*   *   *

Leslie had just left Kings County Hospital and was
walking along Clarkson Avenue when the white Saturn
pulled up to the curb and the man wearing a black ski
mask said, "Get in."

Leslie knew right away that this wasn't a coincidence—David had told her that the man who'd shot
him was wearing a black ski mask and Leslie didn't
hesitate. She knew that the man had Jessica and, putting
her daughter's life first, she got right inside the car.

"Who the hell are you?"

"Easy," the man said. Leslie recognized his voice. It
was the man who had called the other night. "If you
notice, I got a bulge in my winter coat. Not my pants—
though I got one there too—my winter coat. That's a
gun and it's pointed right at you so don't try nothin'."

The man steered the car around a corner, past New
York Avenue.

"Where are we going?"

"To get me my money."

"What money? Didn't you take the money the other
night?"

"I mean the *rest* of my money. You see this piece of shit I'm driving? It's a pussy car—cunts ride this shit. I had to lease it 'cause your old man banged up my LeSabre. He also didn't have the right amount of money in the briefcase, like he was eighteen grand short. Now I want twenty grand and we'll call it a deal."

Leslie didn't know how she was going to get twenty thousand dollars, especially at three o'clock in the afternoon. But she was afraid to say no. What if the man left and this turned out to be her last chance to save Jessica?

"Okay, I'll give you the money," Leslie said, "but first take me to my daughter."

"What do you think I am, stupid?" the man said. "I'll give you your little girl back in one piece, but you gotta get me the money first."

"I'll get you the money," Leslie said. "I promise I will. But it's late. I don't know how I can get it now."

At the next corner, the man made a sharp turn on to a side street and parked the car next to the curb.

"You get me my money now or you get the fuck outta the car."

"Is my daughter alive?"

"Did you hear what I just said?"

"What do you want me to do, go to a cash machine and take out twenty thousand dollars? I need time. Maybe if you'd come to me earlier in the day—"

"Don't give me all this bullshit!"

The man was screaming. Leslie saw the bulge in his jacket and tried to go for it. But the man stopped her, grabbing her arms.

"Not so fast, sweetheart. And you try that again I'll blow your daughter away and tie her up to a cinder block and dump her in the East River. I swear to God I will."

Leslie was crying.

"Please," she pleaded. "What do you want from me?"

"I want twenty grand."

"I don't have it."

"Then get the fuck outta my car and call me when you do."

"How can I call you?"

"Or I'll call you."

Leslie didn't want to take the chance. She couldn't leave now. She had to stay somehow.

"I know," she said, "you can have my car. It's a Mercedes. It's worth at least twenty thousand dollars. It's in my parking lot at home. I can take you to it."

"So the police can come arrest me? No thanks, sweetheart."

"You have to let me see my daughter. Please. You have to."

"I don't have to do shit," the man said. "But I'll make a deal with you. I won't hurt your daughter if you give me something right now."

The man's hand was under Leslie's coat, massaging her stocking-covered thigh. She squeezed her legs together and moved toward the door.

"Don't you dare."

"You seemed to like it a second ago."

"I want to see my daughter this instant."

"I wanted to make a deal with you. You don't seem to want to."

The man tried to put his hand on Leslie's leg again, but Leslie shifted away.

"Why can't you just be a nice guy?" Leslie said. "I don't want you to go to jail. I won't report any of this to the police. You have your money. I'll say you gave us our daughter back and I don't know anything else."

The man lifted the gun again, keeping it low under the dashboard, and pointed it at Leslie's stomach.

"I told you what the deal is," he said. "Now you want to say hello to my friend Dick or don't you?"

With his other hand, the man unzipped his jeans, then slid them off along with his underwear. Maybe it was because she was so close, but it looked like there were two baseballs hanging there.

Leslie's hand was gripping the handle of the door.

"Please," she said. "Why can't you be reasonable?"

"You got ten seconds or you'll never see your little girl again."

"I can't," Leslie said. "Please, I—I'll give you the money. Twenty-*five* thousand. I'll give it to you tomorrow if you just bring me to my daughter."

"Six."

Crying, Leslie pleaded, "Please. Just bring me to my daughter. Bring me to her!"

"Two."

"What the hell is wrong with you?"

The man was pushing Leslie's head down.

"All right," Leslie said desperately, "but not here. Let's go someplace else."

"None of that bullshit," the man said, still trying to push her head down. "Right here, right now."

"This street's too busy," Leslie said. "Someone could come by."

"There's nobody here," the man said.

"Oh yeah? What about her?"

The man turned to look. Thinking about Jessica, knowing this could be her last chance to save her, Leslie lunged across the seat with her right hand and grabbed the man's huge testicles. They were hard and ice-cold.

She squeezed, digging in with her long fingernails. The harder she squeezed, the more likely she'd see Jessica alive. The man was screaming. With her free hand she tried to wrestle away the gun, while her other hand continued to try to crush the man's balls. She managed to get her hand around the handle of the gun and her middle finger near the trigger. Then she steered the gun until it was pointing toward the man's face. The gun fired. A bullet exploded through the man's right eye. Leslie ignored the bloody mess and got a better grip. Four more bullets went into the man's head. When the gun was empty, Leslie kept squeezing the trigger. She felt like she was crying, but she didn't hear any sound. The man was slumped over toward the door—his head a bright red mass. Leslie was staring straight ahead, convulsing. Her right hand was still squeezing those enormous testicles.

Twenty-Two

"IT'S ALL OVER," Dominguez said. "You're under arrest."

He was standing over David's bed at the Rusk Institute of Rehabilitation in Manhattan. David wasn't surprised to see him there. Dominguez had come to see him at least once every day to grill him about Amy Lee. Most of the time, David had managed to stay cool, mainly because he was so high on anti-anxiety medication and painkillers. But this was the first time Dominguez had said he was going to arrest him.

"For what?" David managed to say.

The smell of Dominguez's aftershave was making David nauseous.

"A man came forward," Dominguez said. "He said he was walking by Amy Lee's building on the night of the murder at a little before six p.m. He said he saw you leaving the building, walking fast toward Seventh Avenue South. We showed him a picture of you and he said he'd have no problem identifying you in a lineup."

David was too dazed to think clearly, but he was still positive that Dominguez was bluffing. It had been more than a month since the murder. Why would it have taken so long for a witness to come forward?

"I wasn't there," David said weakly. "How many times do we have to go through this?"

"It's not a matter of what you say or what I say anymore," Dominguez said. "Now it's a matter of facts. I've got my witness and I've got my evidence too. Our lab examined the shoes your wife said you were wearing the night of the murder. They matched up perfectly with the footprints in the snow we found outside of Amy Lee's building."

David knew that this was probably bullshit too. It was snowing so hard that night there couldn't have been footprints.

"I know what you want me to say," David said, "but it's not going to happen. I took the bus home that night. I had nothing to do with any of this."

Now Dominguez sat down on the bed next to David and leaned close to his face. He must have used the whole bottle of aftershave. "Look, cocksucker," he said quietly. "I know you killed that woman. I don't care how many times I have to come here, or how long it takes, but I'm gonna get you to admit it. And I don't give a shit about your little girl or what a victim you are. You're going down for this."

* * *

A week later, David was released from Rusk. Leslie had called to say she wasn't going to come pick him up, even though the hospital was only about forty blocks from their apartment. When he was in the hospital in Brooklyn, Leslie had said she was too traumatized to visit again, but she hadn't visited him in Manhattan either. David was extremely upset, but he didn't want to get into a big fight on the phone.

Leaving the hospital, David had to walk on crutches. The doctors had told him that he would probably have a limp for the rest of his life, and he would have to go to outpatient appointments with a physical therapist for at least the next few weeks.

During the cab ride uptown, David got claustrophobic. He was afraid that he was going to suffocate to death and he cursed his doctor for taking him off his Ativan. He had the driver pull over to the curb and wait several minutes until he caught his breath.

When he came into the apartment, he was hoping there would be a welcome home celebration. Maybe Leslie had invited some friends over and they'd all jump out and yell "Surprise!" But instead the mood was bleak. Leslie's parents had returned to Florida a couple of weeks earlier. Leslie was standing in the vestibule and he almost didn't recognize her.

"Are you okay?"

"Fine," Leslie said without any emotion. "Why?"

"It's just—I don't think I've ever seen you this thin."

"I'm fat," Leslie said seriously. "And I wish you'd just stop commenting about the way I look already because frankly I'm sick of it."

David had to sit down. His hip was still bothering him and the doctor told him he should avoid standing up for long periods of time. But first he wanted to see his daughter.

"Where's Jessica?"

Leslie had gone into the kitchen. The apartment smelled like roast chicken and David heard sizzling frying pans. He limped into the kitchen and repeated the question.

"She's in her room," Leslie said. She was pouring a container of half-and-half into a bowl of mashed potatoes, adding a stick of butter. Then she stirred the concoction with a wooden spoon.

"That's the welcome I get? Not even a peck on the cheek?"

"Look," Leslie said. "I just can't deal with that right now, okay? I really wish you'd just leave me the hell alone."

David cringed, feeling a sharp pain in his hip. He was suddenly weak—the room was spinning.

"Jessica!" David called, limping into the living room. "I'm home!" He waited a few seconds, struggling to take off his shoes, then he called again, "Jessica! Jessica!"

Finally, Jessica came out of her room. Because Leslie had refused to visit him in the hospital, David hadn't seen Jessica since the police had recovered her from William DiStefano's basement in Brooklyn. He barely recognized her. She had lost a lot of weight and had deep, dark circles under her eyes. Her hair was tangled and greasy, as if she hadn't showered in days.

"Come here, princess," David said, trying to act as though he didn't think anything were wrong. "Thank God you're okay."

Jessica remained where she was, staring down at her clenched hands. David leaned forward to try to kiss her, balancing himself on his crutches, but Jessica took a couple of steps backward to avoid him.

"What's wrong, sweetheart?" David said. "Don't you want to say hello to your daddy?"

Leslie came out of the kitchen, holding the wooden spoon.

"Jessica doesn't like to be touched."

"Why not?"

"Because she just doesn't. Does everything need to be repeated to you?"

* * *

Leslie had cooked enough food for ten people. David watched in horror as she stuffed food into her mouth, then rushed into the bathroom to throw up. Jessica was busy meticulously cutting her chicken into small bite-size pieces, but not eating at all. Meanwhile, David was preoccupied with his own worries. Suddenly, he had incredible lower back pain. He was certain that something was wrong with his other kidney—he needed to go on dialysis again. He didn't know how he was going to make it through the night without his Ativan.

Later, lying in bed, the pain was excruciating. At one point, he was convinced he was dying and told Leslie to call the hospital. Leslie told him to "stop acting like a child," and shifted as far to her side of the bed as possible.

All night, David was in a state of high anxiety. He imagined that Dominguez was sitting on the bed next to him, leaning close, and then he saw Amy in the room, pointing a gun at him, her face dripping with blood. Then Amy turned into William DiStefano, wearing his black ski mask, laughing in that sick way. The vision was so terrifying that he rolled over to Leslie's side of the bed and put an arm around her bony body.

"Get off me," Leslie said seriously. She was wide awake.

David lay on his back the rest of the night. His head started itching and he feared that the rest of his hair was falling out. Then he couldn't stop thinking about his heartbeat. It was getting faster and faster and he was convinced something was wrong with his kidney. He was dying and no one was going to do anything to save him. Then he saw himself—in that parking lot again, running toward his car. He heard the three gunshots and saw his body collapsing on to the ground. Then he was in Amy Lee's kitchen. She had just fallen and he

picked up the frying pan. He swung it against her head
again and again.

* * *

The next morning, the *Times* reported a break in the
Amy Lee murder case. The police had discovered that
the gun found at the scene had been used in an
unsolved homicide on Amy's block last year. Now they
were linking Amy Lee to that murder and investigating
whether a friend of the dead man—a drug dealer who'd
been wanted on sexual assault charges—may have
killed Amy in revenge. Police still weren't sure whether
there was any connection between Amy and William
DiStefano, the man who'd allegedly kidnapped Jessica
Sussman outside of her school in Manhattan and kept
her tied up in the basement of his apartment in
Brooklyn, but they were leaning toward the theory that
DiStefano had acted alone.

David wasn't relieved. He knew that this was just a
theory, probably one of many theories that the police
were working on. He knew that Dominguez would be
back to grill him, and that he would keep grilling him,
trying to get him to break down. And even if the police
did wind up pinning the murder on someone else, it
wouldn't be reason to celebrate. No matter what
happened, he was still a murderer and he was going to
have to live with that for the rest of his life. He just
didn't think he deserved any more suffering.

He went into the kitchen on his crutches. Food was
cooking on every burner and Leslie was maniacally
stirring two pots at once.

"Here," David said, putting the newspaper that was
opened to the Amy Lee article on the counter for her to

read. "In case you still thought I might be a killer."

Leslie glanced at the article, then went back to her cooking without saying anything.

"You know, I don't know what the hell you think this is accomplishing?" David said. "You want to divorce me? Go ahead! Don't do me any favors!"

David staggered out, past the dining room, then came back into the kitchen.

"And why the hell is the table set for four places?"

Leslie didn't answer.

"Did you hear what I just said? Am I talking to the goddamn walls in this apartment?!"

"We're having company," Leslie said.

"Really?" David said. "You'd think you'd let me know about something like that. What is this, my belated welcome home party?"

"No, it's a party for Maureen," Leslie said quietly. "She had some good news last week. She's pregnant."

* * *

There was only one thing about this whole pregnancy that didn't make sense to Joey. Maureen said the kid would be coming sometime in November and Joey did the math and figured out this meant she must've been knocked up sometime in February. But this didn't make sense to him because he couldn't remember screwing Maureen in February. When they screwed last week it was the first time in a few months, and a couple of days after that Maureen said the baby was coming.

But Joey just decided there were probably a lot of things about women he'd never understand. Maybe it was possible to have an eight-month pregnancy. Or maybe it was some of his old cum, festering in there that got to her. It was no use busting his chops about it with everything else in his life going so good. He had a new cabling job, his debts were clear—thanks to a few winners at the track—and he had action on the NCAA tournament. What else could a man ask for?

When they arrived at the Sussmans' for dinner, right away Joey noticed something was different. It looked like the waiting room in a hospital. Maureen had said that there was something wrong with Leslie, that she had some kind of woman's disease, and that David was going to be sick for the rest of his life. But Joey didn't understand why Maureen was blaming herself for all of this. She was going to church every day, talking about how everything was all her fault. Joey still thought there might be some pills or something she could take.

For once, there was some good food to eat at the Sussmans'. No more health food shit or ordering in Chinese—Leslie had cooked up a four-course roast beef and potato dinner and Joey dug in, enjoying every bite. There wasn't much talking. Maureen just kept mumbling to herself about Jesus and Leslie kept stuffing her mouth then getting up to go to the bathroom. David just sat there with a dumb look on his face. But the best part of the night was that at the end of the meal there was no stupid kiddy show. Everybody just sat around, eating chocolate cake and drinking coffee, not saying a word. Joey wished that every night at the Sussmans' could be this perfect.